Embarrassed to Be with Amy

John Cheek

Copyright © 2022 John Cheek
All rights reserved
First Edition

NEWMAN SPRINGS PUBLISHING
320 Broad Street
Red Bank, NJ 07701

First originally published by Newman Springs Publishing 2022

ISBN 978-1-68498-067-3 (Paperback)
ISBN 978-1-68498-068-0 (Digital)

Printed in the United States of America

Chapter 1

Hot Sauce

It was November in the Lone Star state of Texas. While relaxing in his apartment, Maleek's cell phone started ringing. He glanced at the caller ID on his cell phone's screen. It was his mother, Daloris, calling him, better known as Momma D. He picked up the phone. "Hello." Hearing the tone of her voice, he knew she was extremely angry with him.

"Boy! It's one ten already. I told yo narrow ass to be here at 1:00 p.m. I wanted the whole family to take pictures before Thanksgiving dinner."

"Mother, you must not refer to me as a boy. The White man has used that word to keep Black men within an inferior mind state."

"Look here, boy. I done cooked the collard greens just how you like them. I done fried the turkey and the ham. I baked the sweet potatoes with marshmallows on top of them. I also baked the macaroni with three layers of cheese."

"Didn't I just tell you not to call me a boy? Plus, you know I don't eat pork anymore," he replied assertively in a loud tone of voice.

"You thumb-sucking, nappy-head little troll. Who in the magic Martian you think you're raising your voice at, boy? You've been brainwashed ever since you got out of prison. I told yo ass that I don't want to hear that pro-Black shit. Your little punk ass never lived in the sixties. How dare you talk to me like that."

"I'm sorry, Momma, I didn't mean to."

She was enraged. "Boy! If you don't get your wannabe Malcom X butt to Irving, I'll break a long-pointed stick off a tree and paint it white. Then I will whip yo ass with it before it dries off. Every slash I strike you with gone leave a permanent white scar on your back. Then you'll be walking around here looking like a zebra that was attacked by a hyena. Now get your behind to Irving," she demanded.

Maleek began to reminisce on the past when Momma D used to spank him when he was a kid. She would pour hot sauce on a stick from a tree, then whip him butt naked in front of his sister and friends. While holding the phone, he was silent. All of a sudden, he began to tremble as he remembered being beaten by his mom. "Yes, ma'am, I'm leaving now."

"That's my little boy," she replied in a settled voice.

"I'm not eating no pork, though," he replied.

"You gone eat whatever I put on your plate."

"But, Mom."

She became angry again. "'But Mom' my Black ass. What'd I tell you about talking back? Don't feel that you're too old for a butt whipping. Now don't give me any more back talk. It only takes twenty minutes to get to Irving from Arlington. You better be here at one thirty-five. If you're one minute late, I'm going to stick my foot up your black hole. Do you understand me, boy?"

"Yes, Mother," answered Maleek.

"Good, that's what I want to hear. And don't wear that cutoff leg stocking with the holes in it on your head."

"It's not a stocking. It's a kufi."

"Whatever, Mohammed."

"Peace and blessings be upon him," he said in a quick blurt.

"Do what, boy?"

"Nothing, Mom. I'm on my way, goodbye."

"Bye, boy, hurry up." The two of them hung up their phones, ending the conversation.

His friend Romme had just finished rolling up a marijuana cigar. He then grabbed a lighter off the table set in the living room. "You wanna puff, puff? Before you leave," he asked as he held the blunt in the air.

"You know damn well that Momma D will smell that weed on me. You knavish misfit, you must want me to catch a beatdown." Maleek grabbed his car keys and walked toward the front door.

"Why is your momma so mean? Was she raised by Candy Man and Cruella?"

Maleek gawked at him. "I don't know. Just like we don't know why yo momma look like Jeepers Creepers," he answered.

"Ha!" shouted Romme as he was exiting the doorway. Maleek paused in the middle of the doorway and looked at him. With a smirk on his face, Romme blew smoke out his mouth toward Maleek.

"What do you want, you baboon's ass?" said Maleek.

"You remember when yo momma beat yo ass with that stick? In front of me and the rest of our friends when we were young? Hot sauce was flying everywhere like a house painter on crystal meth." He giggled after asking that humiliating question. "Then a dog came out of nowhere and started licking hot sauce off your butt cheeks. You couldn't even stop it." Romme chuckled as he slumped down in the sofa holding his tummy.

The laughter got louder and louder. With an angry facial expression, Maleek cursed, "Goddammit, Romme." Holding the doorknob with his right hand, his right arm started shaking. He quickly clutched his right wrist with his left hand, stopping the shaking. "Goddammit, Romme. You know better than to bring up that horrible event. You gone make me have epilepsy. Then I'm gone have a seizure. You know that shit is like PTSD."

Laughter was the only reply. With an upside-down smile on his face, Maleek exited the apartment, slamming the door behind him. His friend's laughter was heard outside the apartment building.

Chapter 2

Head on Wheels

Maleek hopped into his car, then backed out the parking space and began to drive. He came to a standstill in front of the exit gate of the apartment complex. His vehicle triggered the sensor to the automatic gate. It slowly began to open to let him through. While the gate was opening, he began recalling his mother thrashing him in front of his friends.

He vividly recaptured the scene in his imagination. He recalled holding his private part with his left hand. Momma D was gripping his right wrist tightly while hitting him with a stick in her other hand. Ten of his friends were in the background, pointing and laughing. One of his friends was laughing so hard he had an asthma attack. Also watching the spectacle was his sister Tawanna and her friend Amy. Amy was the only one not laughing. She always liked Maleek but kept her feelings secret. As Momma D struck him again and again, his knees were reaching his chin as if he was high-stepping like an NFL player at football practice. His Irving Boys Football Association coach would be impressed with his footwork.

Bang! Bang! Maleek jumped, startled. Somebody knocked on his driver-side window, snapping him out of his trance. He glanced to his left, then rolled down his window. It was Troy, a friend who lived in the same apartment complex.

"What's up, brother man? You going to work today? If so, what's up with a hookup? It's Thanksgiving. I'm hungry, bro."

"Why would I drive to my job when it's only a minute's walk away from my apartment? Romme just bought a weed sack from you. For once, how about you pay for your food, you bugga boo?"

"Come on, bro. Why do you gotta be like that? It's Thanksgiving, for crying out loud," replied Troy. Maleek stared at him with an upside-down smile. His bottom lip was poking out further than his top lip.

"Thanksgiving! That's the problem with you brothas now n' days. Celebrating a fake holiday made by the White man."

"Aw! Shit! Here comes Brother May I with his pro-Black speech."

"What! You just call me Brother May I? Well, maybe you should soak up this knowledge I'm trying to teach you. Then you wouldn't have the IQ of a mountain goat. While you are standing here outside my car window like a hobo begging for food, how 'bout you go collect some cans and eat them, Mr. Billy Goat?"

Troy had a grin on his face. "If I listen to your wisdom, you must give. Will you hook me up later tonight?" he asked, rolling his eyes.

"Why you roll your eyes like that?"

"I didn't roll my eyes."

"Bro, yes, you did. Are calling me a liar?" Troy didn't respond. He kept looking at him with a blank face. "I'm not giving you nothing, you nincompoop. Move back so I can drive off," said Maleek.

"Wait! I'll listen," insisted Troy.

"I want more than you just giving me your undivided attention."

"What more can I give right now?" wondered Troy.

"Next time I buy a weed sack from you, this future sack best be as fat as your Auntie Joy. My sack better not be skimpy. That last bag you gave me was skinnier than an anorexic model on cocaine."

"I promise I'll hook it up," assured Troy.

"Okay, I'll hook you up next time I'm at work. As far as Thanksgiving. If you were Native American, and your ancestors helped the pilgrims survive a new land, showed them how to plant crops, showed them the land, instead of being grateful these Europeans gave them blankets with smallpox on them. Almost killed off all the buffalo, then took their land. Thanksgiving, my ass. Yo

Black ass running around here talking about Happy Thanksgiving. Damn fool." Maleek sped off laughing.

Troy quickly jumped backward, keeping his feet from being run over. *Why I got to be a fool?* he thought to himself.

Realizing he had wasted time chatting with Troy, Maleek drove fast to make it to his mother's house on time for Thanksgiving. Speeding in the middle lane, he happened to quickly glance to his left. He had seen the back of a woman in the car ahead with long hair leaning over to the driver seat.

On purpose, he decelerated to watch this mysterious woman give her man oral sex. The guy in the driver seat had one hand on the steering wheel. The other hand was gripped on the back of the passenger's head. The driver quickly looked over to his right. He saw Maleek gradually peeping back and forth through the window, then back to the road while driving. Maleek smiled and gave him a thumbs-up.

The driver smiled back, then removed his right palm off the passenger. He returned a thumbs-up. Suddenly, he began to pant. The feeling from receiving a blow job was showing in his facial expression. The driver rolled down the passenger window from his door panel. Maleek cut off his radio so he could hear the driver moaning. The sound of traffic made it difficult to hear. "Ah!" shouted the driver as he busted a nut.

Maleek grinned. He anxiously waited for the woman to raise her head. He wanted to see her face. The passenger rose quickly, then spat the sperm out the window. It was another man. Maleek was fooled by the long hair. Braff! Maleek threw up in his lap; he wiped his mouth off. "Son of a bitch," he cursed. He sped up, losing sight of the homosexuals. *Goddammit, that's what I get for being nosy,* he thought to himself.

Smelling like vomit, he was now entering Irving city limits. He exited Highway 360 onto Freeway 183, then Beltline Road. *I can't believe I threw up on myself,* he thought.

He drove down Beltline Road for a minute, then turned right onto Walnut Hill. About two hundred yards down Walnut Hill, he made another right turn. His parents moved into an upscale neighborhood that was built around 2001–02. A very small, secluded area, mostly two-story houses.

Both of Maleek's parents had gone to college. His mother had earned her master's degree in business. She owned her own dentistry and became a dentist herself. His dad earned his master's degree in criminal justice. He became a hard-nosed prosecutor. Both of his parents were very prominent people in life.

Maleek pulled up to his parents' house, parking in the street. Next to the curb, while cutting off his engine, he spotted Amy getting out of her car. She was carrying her luggage inside. She stood about five foot seven or eight, approximately weighing a 155 to 170, he guessed. She was what a Black man would consider a thick-looking woman. She was thick in all the right places. She had long black hair with green eyes. She was prettier than spring before summer.

Maleek hadn't seen her since they were in high school. His sister Tawanna and Amy were best friends. After high school, most of his childhood friends went to college or the Army. At the age of eighteen, Maleek went to prison for bank robbery. He still claimed his innocence to this day.

Chapter 3

Yuke

Amy was twenty-four; she had just earned her master's degree in psychology. She was currently moving her luggage into her parents' house. Right now, her parents were out of town for Thanksgiving. As she entered the house with luggage, Maleek went unnoticed as he watched her from his car. In a hurry, he got out of his automobile, then made a dash to the front door of his parents' house.

When she came back outside to get more bags out of her vehicle, she saw a glimpse of Maleek. He was already opening the front door. She had seen him but didn't recognize him. He had gotten bigger during his stint in prison. He was a very handsome young man. He stood five eleven in height, weighed 195 pounds. He was ripped up and had long braids. He was twenty-four years of age.

He didn't want her to see him and try to chat with him. He had been biased since getting out of prison. Plus, he was embarrassed of the puke on his lap. The time was 1:33 p.m. when he made it inside his parents' house.

"There goes my oldest boy. Boy, if you were two more minutes late, I was literally going to stick my foot up your ass. If you don't believe me, there goes my steel-toe boots right there," said Momma D as she pointed at the boots. They were bright, highly polished. The glare damn near blinded him when he looked.

"I polished them good to just make sure the tip of the boot makes a smooth entrance in yo ass," said Tyrone, his dad.

Momma D and Tyrone were always giving Maleek a hard time. They treat him like an outcast of the family. They all felt distinguished in the fact that the entire family was pious and successful. They saw Maleek as the black sheep of the family. His younger brother Brandon, along with Tawanna, his two siblings, treated him the same way. Brandon was a part of the United States Army. Tawanna was a nurse and an intern. She was studying to be a doctor. Maleek was the oldest of the three.

His granddad Willbe stayed neutral in the matter concerning Maleek to the whole family. He was the alpha male. He was a retired doctor. Grandma Auatta usually sided with Momma D. She never really said much. She just agreed with her on any subject matter, only because she wanted to fit in. She would never admit that Maleek was her favorite grandson. She was a retired nurse.

Uncle Roy and his wife, Janeen, were both lawyers. They loved Maleek unconditionally. The two of them always took up for him in family feuds. Their son and daughter, Anthony and Nicole, also loved him very much. Neither one would judge him for his past. Both studied law in college.

Aunt Abby felt the same way about Maleek as her sister and Tyrone. Aunt Abby was a college teacher; she instructed government. Her husband, Nat, owned a car shop. He was a very skilled mechanic. He thought Maleek was a bad influence on Shanna and Jojo, his children. Jojo studied business management in college. Shanna was a senior in high school. They didn't talk to Maleek much, only because their parents wouldn't allow them to.

"Man! I was hoping that you'd be late. I wanted to see Momma stick her boot up your behind," said Tawanna. Momma D, Tyrone, and Tawanna were all standing close to Maleek in that order. They hadn't noticed the vomit on his clothes yet. They were too busy dogging him. Uncle Roy rose off the sofa and headed their way.

"Get out of my way, you three egg-stealing weasels. How is it that you three all talk crazy to him without even greeting him like family," said Uncle Roy as he scrambled through them to hug Maleek. Knowing he had puke on him, he intentionally dodged Uncle Roy and hugged Momma D tightly.

"What's that smell?" said Tyrone. Maleek moved away from Momma D. Uncle Roy, with his arms held up in a hugging stance, tried to hug his nephew a second time. He dipped under him, juking him like a running back.

"What in the world. How is you gone hug these heifers before your favorite uncle?" said Roy. While gripping his dad firmly in a hug, Maleek turned his head to his left, looked at Uncle Roy, and winked. Uncle Roy smiled back, wondering what he was up to. Maleek let go of Tyrone, then hugged his sister quickly.

"I didn't want no hug from you, loser! Get off me," demanded Tawanna. He released her. "What's that on your shirt? It's on your pants too."

"Oh! I forgot to mention that I threw up on the way here," lied Maleek.

Granddad Willbe laughed out loud from the living room sofa. The rest of the family began to giggle too, except the three who had contracted vomit on their clothes.

"That's what that smell was. Goddammit, Maleek, now I have to change clothes," said Tyrone.

"Thanks a lot, son. I need to change clothes too. You always fucking up something," shouted Momma D. She and Tyrone went to change clothes. He had a big grin on his face.

"You did that on purpose, you jerk. I don't have any clothes to change into, you asshole," cursed Tawanna.

Chapter 4

Hug

"Momma and Daddy aren't here to protect you right now. You're a hyena slipping in a lion's realm," said Maleek. He held his arms up, acting like a lion as he roared loudly.

"What's that supposed to mean? I'm not scared of... Ah!" she yelled as she tried to run. He grabbed her, then wrestled her down to the ground. She lay on her stomach, struggling to get up. He held her down and brushed his pukey clothes all over her. She screamed loudly again.

"Boy! Get off your sister," shouted Aunt Abby. Maleek smiled, sitting on the floor holding her at bay. He slapped her on the back of her head then stood up.

"I can't stand you, boy!" shouted Tawanna as she stood up.

"Well, sweetheart, I would give you a hug, but you have vomit all over you," said Grandma Auatta. The rest of the family waved at him, greeting him. They felt the same way Grandma Auatta did.

"What you gone do about those clothes?" asked Uncle Roy.

"I'll change into some of Brandon's clothes," answered Maleek. Brandon, his younger brother, was twenty-one, three years younger than him. Brandon was bigger and taller than his older brother, Maleek. While off tour with the Army, he lived with his parents. He was on his way back home now to join the family for Thanksgiving. Maleek went to his younger brother's room and changed clothes. He came back into the living room with clean clothes on.

All his relatives hugged him and talked to him briefly. All the men sat down in the living room, watching Thursday Thanksgiving football. All the women went to the kitchen to finish cooking dinner. "When Brandon gets here, we'll be ready to take pictures," said Momma D.

Ten minutes later, Brandon walked through the front door. A White woman trailed in behind him. One by one, the entire family greeted him with open arms. Maleek was last to hug his little brother. Tawanna didn't hug him due to the vomit on her clothes.

"Well, well, if it isn't the scum bucket convict," trash-talked Brandon. Maleek couldn't believe that after all these years, his younger brother would talk down to him. When he released him from the hug, his smile turned upside down.

"Well, if it isn't the Uncle Tom fighting for his slave master and pleasing his she-devil," countered Maleek with an insult.

"Ha!" muttered Becky in shock as she crossed her arms in anger.

"Boy! Go sit yo ass down on the sofa. Your younger brother is a hero," said Momma D. Maleek walked away and sat down on the couch. Uncle Roy covered his mouth with his hand, trying to conceal his laughter. "Hi, honey, I'm Momma D. You must be Becky. Brandon told me all about you." She and the rest of the family greeted Brandon's girlfriend.

Becky followed all the ladies to the kitchen; all the guys went into the living room. Before the two groups could fully separate, Brandon asked, "How come you didn't hug me, Tawanna?"

"Your dick-in-the-booty, ex-con brother got puke all over me," replied Tawanna.

"Oh! I seen Amy when I was coming in the house. She told me to tell you and everybody else hi. She didn't want to call and interrupt our holiday."

"What! My best friend is here." With an excited look on her face, she pulled her cell phone out of her pants pocket. In a rush, she dialed Amy's phone number. "You're outside getting the rest of your luggage? I'm coming outside now." Tawanna ran outside, thrilled to see her best friend again.

All the men walked into the living room and sat down. The women strolled into the kitchen. Momma D's cell phone rung. "Hello," said Momma D as she answered her phone.

"Momma! Amy's parents went out of town for Thanksgiving. May I invite her to our house for Thanksgiving?" asked Tawanna over the phone.

"Of course, Amy is always welcomed over here," answered Momma D. "Hurry up and get back here. We're almost ready to take pictures then eat dinner."

"Okay, we're coming back now." Two minutes later, Tawanna, followed by Amy, entered the house. She led her best friend to the living room first. Maleek was sitting next to his cousin, Anthony, Roy's son. All the women came out of the kitchen into the living room.

"Goddammit! She's fine," whispered Anthony.

"Don't be entertained by that White devil. Stick to the sistas, our ebony queens," whispered Maleek.

"Ain't nothing wrong with a little White chocolate. You know what I'm saying, cuz," he replied. Maleek gave him a funny look as his cousin popped a Tic Tac in his mouth.

The whole family greeted Amy, except Maleek. "Tawanna, you changed clothes. That's a very beautiful dress. You went to the store that quick and bought that dress?" assumed Momma D.

"No, Amy let me borrow it. My other set of clothes are in the washing machine, at her house," said Tawanna.

"Look at you, girl. You used to be skinny as Olive Oyl from *Popeye*. You grew up to be an amazing-looking woman. I bet all the men be chasing you like a pack of prison guards led by some hound dogs on a fresh scented trail of an escaped jailbird."

"Thank you, Momma D, for the very descriptive childhood memories. I see everyone here, except Maleek," said Amy.

"Speaking of jailbird, there he goes right there," said Tawanna, pointing. Amy's face lit up with excitement. Her eyeballs followed Tawanna's finger with her. He was sitting on the couch while everyone else was embracing Amy. With a frown on his face, he had his arms crossed, displaying a bad mood.

"Hi, Maleek," said Amy as she waved at him. "It's nice to see you after all these years. Happy Thanksgiving."

"Yeah, whatever. I don't celebrate this made-up holiday by the White man," replied Maleek.

"Boy! If you don't get your sorry tail off that sofa and acknowledge her, I'll pull my high heel off and stab your ass," yelled Momma D.

"Don't be so mean, Maleek," said Grandma Auatta. He rose off the couch and put out his hand in a balled-up fist to dap hands with her. Amy reached out to dap him.

Wham! "Give that damn girl a hug," ordered Momma D after smacking him upside the back of his head. She slapped him so hard he almost headbutted Amy. He did as he was commanded. While hugging her, her sweet scent enticed him. His hard, cut-up buff body fascinated her.

"Wow, you've gotten so big," said Amy as she held him tightly. Maleek gently disbanded their cuddling. Despite his heart feeling warm next to her, his racially biased mind shut that natural feeling down.

"That's usually what happens to ex-cons when they leave prison. They either get fat, or swoll," stereotyped Tawanna.

"That's why you called him a jailbird. What were you convicted for, Maleek?" asked Amy.

"Bank robbery, but I didn't do it. Like most Black men, I was wrongly sentenced in the Anglo-American courts. I was innocent," Maleek explained.

Tyrone was very angry out of nowhere. "You're a lie! You did it, now admit it like a man!"

"He was innocent! And you knew it!" yelled Uncle Roy with fury.

Amy was confused. "Why would y'all disagree about the verdict?"

Chapter 5

Testify

Before his dad or his uncle could answer her question, Maleek raised his hand in the air as if waiting on a teacher to call upon him. He caught everyone's attention; silence filled the room. He inhaled a long, deep breath. Then let out a long, deep sigh of sorrow. He covered his mouth with his other hand as he prepared himself to speak. His eyes became watery.

Amy specialized in psychology. She could tell that he was going through a mental and emotional process. "I'm…I'm going…I'm…," stuttered Maleek as he panted, wheezing and gasping rapidly with his breath. He was trying not to cry. She patted him on his back.

"It's okay, take your time to explain yourself." He took another deep breath, then moved his hand off his mouth.

"They're disagreeing because Uncle Roy was my lawyer. Daddy prosecuted me," wept Maleek. He swiftly snuggled Amy, then sniffled and sobbed heavily on her right shoulder. With his face resting on her shoulder, she felt his tears pouring out.

"It's okay, darling," said Amy. The whole family could hear his pain as he whimpered on Amy's shoulder loudly. He couldn't hold his anguish anymore. While embracing him, she rubbed his back.

"Look what you did, Tyrone. You Uncle Tom jigaboo," said Uncle Roy in an outrage. Amy glanced at Tyrone while holding Maleek in her arms. She shook her head from side to side in disappointment.

"I was just trying to teach him accountability for his actions," said Tyrone.

"He never let me tell my side of the story," said Maleek, crying on Amy.

"Would you like to explain what happened right here?" asked Amy. "That way, you can tell your dad how you feel."

"Yes," uttered Maleek, shedding tears.

"We don't have time for his sad story. We need to take family pictures," said Momma D.

"What you're going to do is shut your pie hole," said Granddad Willbe. "Then we're going to let my grandson explain himself. Do you understand me, you rhinoceros's belly?"

"Huh!" mumbled Momma D in shock. She then looked at her belly. "Daddy!"

"Daddy my ass! Now hush up! Before I whip off my belt and beat you like a thief in the Middle East!" Half the family began to snicker quietly.

"Yeah! That's right! Be silent, you camel's tongue! Take the floor, nephew, express yourself," shouted Uncle Roy.

"It was getting close to the end of the month. I had already paid my half of the rent. Romme needed to borrow some money to pay his half. He said he would pay me back. I told him I would give it to him." Maleek paused, then moaned.

"Take your time," insisted Amy as she patted him on the back.

Tawanna put her mouth close to Brandon's ear. "Look at him, he's supposed to be a gangsta. He over there crying like a little bitch," she whispered. Brandon giggled as Maleek began to tell his story.

"I told Romme to remind me in the morning. He had to be at work during the night, though. So instead of verbally reminding me, he left a note on the table. It read, 'Just leave the money on the table and I'll get it.' I folded the letter up, then stuffed it in my wallet next to my credit card. I left my apartment on my way to the bank. The drive-through and the ATM machine outside was swamped with people. I figured I would make a withdrawal inside the bank. I greeted the teller, then asked her to make a withdrawal with my credit card. I opened my wallet to pull out my credit card.

A few other cards along with the note that Romme left me accidently fell out my wallet. The cards fell to the ground. Amazingly, the note landed on the cabinet. I didn't know it fell out. I bent down to the ground to pick up my fallen credit cards. After placing them back in my wallet, I stood back up to face the teller. She had a bag of money in her hand. I thought nothing of it. I figured she was multitasking or something. I extended my hand to her to give her my card. She gave me the bag full of money without taking my card. I held it to my face. 'What's this?' I asked.

"'You got what you wanted. I have a family, please leave,' shouted the teller, drawing attention.

"I didn't know that she picked up the note and read it during the time I was retrieving my fallen cards from the floor. She thought I was robbing the bank. I asked her, 'What are you are talking about, you feeble-minded child? I didn't ask for this. Take it back.' Just as I was trying to give it back to her, *boom!* The police busted in the bank with guns drawn."

"Place your hands in the air, then slowly face me," ordered the police.

"For some reason, I knew they were talking to me. I followed their command. As I faced them with my hands in the air, the money bag was only about a foot away from my face. *Pow!* The dye pack exploded, making contact with my face, burning my eyes, nose, and mouth. I fell to the ground screaming. The cops pounced on me like a pack of wolves, then handcuffed me. I was completely blinded with the dye pack on my face. I looked like a clown as the authorities dragged me out of the bank. All the people were clapping and cheering like a terrorist had just been caught."

"What happened at your trial?" asked Amy.

"The judge believed my story when Romme testified that he had written the letter. He was going to dismiss the case, but my dad refused to let me off. He almost convinced the judge to give me seven years. Uncle Roy got the judge to agree with a year's probation. My stubborn father wouldn't quit."

"Mr. Johnson, that note does not contain your son's handwriting. When viewing the video film, it's apparent that it was an accident when the note fell out of his wallet. His friend testified on his behalf, vouching for the letter. The teller also testified. She knew your son for years as a nice customer who has been using her bank for years. She openly admits that she made a mistake. Not only that, but your son has also never gotten into any trouble: not in elementary school, or junior high, nor high school. He has a job, and he's enrolled in college," explained the magistrate.

"Your Honor, out of twenty-five years as a renowned prosecutor, I have never lost a case. I will not lose one today. You know me as a very smart man, Your Honor," replied Tyrone.

"Why yes, I would say so, Mr. Johnson."

"Knowing this, that young man over there is my son. That means he has my genes. He is clever, also very cunning. Wouldn't you think so, Your Honor?"

The judge looked at him, then his son. Maleek's bottom lip hung out more than his tucked-in upper lip as he stared at his dad. "Just where are you going with this, Mr. Johnson?"

"Well, Your Honor, today, that thug over there is not my son! He may have my wits, but he used them to commit a crime! Must have got it from his mother. He carefully planned that robbery to get easy results." Momma D gave her husband a look of disgust.

"I object, Your Honor," shouted Uncle Roy as he stood.

"Objection overruled," replied the chief justice.

"As I was saying, Your Honor. That hoodlum over there carefully planned that 211. Don't let him outsmart this courtroom or your reputation, Your Honor. Don't let him make a fool out of me or you. I want the maximum sentence imposed by law on this sneaking, diabolic swindler. I'm requesting sixty months in a federal prison," demanded Tyrone.

The judge looked at him, then rubbed his chin.

He then lifted the small mallet. "I sentence the defendant to thirty-six months." *Wham!* The judge slammed the gavel.

"How did this event change your perception of your father?" asked Amy.

"He was my hero, until that day in court, when he proved that he loved his job more than his family," explained Maleek.

"Mr. Johnson, would you like to say anything to your son right now?"

Tyrone had a mad look on his face. "Yes, I still believe you did it. You soulless, bloodsucking leech."

"How can you be so heartless?" shouted Uncle Roy.

"I need to check on the food. It's two twenty already," said Momma D as she stormed into the kitchen.

Chapter 6

The Plan

"We'll discuss this situation in a more private setting," asserted Amy. Everyone dispersed in their own direction. Maleek wiped his tears away, then went to the bathroom in the hallway. He opened the door. Before he could close it, Amy stopped it from shutting. "Feel free to chat with me at any time." He nodded his head okay, then closed the door. She went back to the living room and sat on the sofa.

She wondered why he didn't ask for her phone number. Tawanna sat next to her. Amy asked her for her brother's cell phone number. She gave it to her. "Look, Amy, I know you like Maleek. Just be careful with him. He's not the same person you knew when we were young," said Tawanna.

"Explain what you mean," replied Amy.

"After his release from prison, he's been acting racist. He seems like a radical Muslim."

"I'm a psychologist, I can help him. Plus, I always liked him since we were younger. He's just angry. He needs someone to talk to."

"Just be cautious, girl. Don't want to see your heart broken."

"You remember when we were younger? We always acted like sisters. Your Barbie doll was my niece, and mine was your niece. If your brother and I can become a happy couple, we would really be sisters by law. You would be my child's aunt," she explained excitedly.

Tawanna thought deeply about this. She smiled, then giggled and hugged Amy.

"If you had a girl, she would be such a good niece. I love that idea, but it's really up to Maleek."

"I can soften him up. Will you help me with him?"

"Of course, let me know what I need to do."

"For starters, be kind and nice to him."

"All right, everybody, let's go outside so we can take pictures," shouted Momma D. Maleek just came out of the restroom. He followed everyone outside to the front yard.

Tawanna and Amy were last, trailing everybody outside. "After we finish eating dinner, ask Maleek to come over to my house. I got a heavy suitcase in my car. We'll have him carry it inside my house. Once we get it inside, I want you to compliment me on my butt," explained Amy.

"Compliment you on your butt! How am I supposed to do that?" wondered Tawanna.

"I'll walk ahead of y'all two in order to open the door. Once I place my key in the lock, be like, 'Hm! Girl, you sure got a big butt for a White girl.' Then ask Maleek for his opinion. We all know that Black men love a big rear. Sir Mix-a-Lot said so, huh."

"Girl, you do have a big ass. How did you get so thick?"

"My dad has always been skinny, but my mom has always been chunky. For some reason, skinny men and fat women always attract one another. Why? I'm not sure. That's like asking why there is a moon and sun. As I grew older my mother's genes kicked in. During college, I worked out a lot too. I did so many squats."

"Tawanna! Amy! We're waiting on you two. Come on so we can eat dinner," demanded Momma D. As the two of them were exiting the house, *wham!*

"Haha!" laughed Amy. "Stop it, you're going to make me blush. Then I'll turn red." After smacking her on the butt, Tawanna giggled, then followed behind her out the house.

Momma D directed everybody where she wanted them to stand. They all bunched up together. Momma D set the camera angle to her satisfaction. Pressing a button on the automatic camera left her ten seconds to join the portrait. She slowly trotted to her spot next to her husband. "Smile, everyone," ordered Momma D. Everyone smiled.

After the first picture, the family, including Becky and Amy, took additional pictures.

All the women took a photo together. When done, all the men gathered together. Brandon and Maleek were in the middle of the group, standing next to one another. "Ha! You have on my clothes," mumbled Brandon.

"After we finish eating, I'll take them off," replied Maleek.

"Smile, you two. Talk after this snapshot," shouted Momma D standing in front of the camera. They both stopped looking at each other and smiled at the camera. She pressed the button; the flash captured the photo. "We're done. Let's eat."

"You're going to remove them clothes off your tail now," shouted Brandon.

"My clothes will be dry soon, there in the dryer. I'll change once we're done eating," replied Maleek.

"That's not my problem. Besides, wet clothes won't hurt you."

"Chill out, little bro, you are tripping," he replied as he rubbed the back of his head.

Brandon slapped his hand away from his head. "I might be younger than you, but I'm bigger. We're not young anymore. I'll wrestle you down to the ground and take those clothes." As the entire family was walking in the house, they came to a standstill; their attention was focused on Maleek and Brandon. "You think because you're bigger, taller, and you're in the Army, you can handle your big brother," said Maleek.

"If you two don't get in this—!" Momma D was interrupted by her husband.

"Hold on, sweetie, let them two wrestle it out. Brandon gone take him down," predicted Tyrone.

Uncle Roy pulled some money out of his pocket. "Put your money where your mouth is. I got two hundred on Maleek," he said, extending his fist to his brother.

"You ain't said nothing but a word, you jive turkey. I got two hundred on Brandon," retorted Tyrone as he dapped hands with Roy. The two brothers were standing face-to-face in the middle of the lawn. Everybody else was watching.

"I'm giving you a chance to do like I told you. Don't make me take you down," threatened Brandon.

Maleek reached out and pinched his younger brother on the cheek. "You're so cute," he taunted.

"You sure you want to do this? You know what kind of training we do in the Army?"

"In prison, I would have made you make me a cup of coffee every morning, boy!" He softly slapped his younger brother across the face, tempting him.

"That's it, come on." The two of them began to walk in a circle. Brandon had a serious look on his face; Maleek had a devious grin on his face. The rest of the family started cheering. Half the family rallied behind Brandon; the other half was encouraging Maleek.

The two of them locked arms like professional wrestlers. As they struggled back and forth, trying to gain leverage on one another, Maleek released his grip on Brandon, then swiftly dipped under his left armpit. He placed his brother in the full nelson. Somehow, Brandon slipped out of the full nelson. He clutched Maleek's right wrist while doing so. As he twisted his right arm, he spun him around. He was now bending Maleek's right arm inward from behind while forcing his hand into the middle of his back, stretching his wrist, bending his arm as his elbow pointed out. He held his brother at bay with this painful move. "Tap out now, or I'll snap your arm like a twig," warned Brandon.

"Never," retorted Maleek. He then shoved his right leg in between Brandon's legs. He bent forward, then swept his leg forward, thrusting up against his capture's right ankle, causing him to lose his balance. Brandon let go of Maleek's arm. As Brandon stumbled backward, Maleek turned around and dashed at him. Just as he caught his balance, Maleek tackled him to the ground. Brandon wrapped his left arm around his neck and squeezed. As Maleek lay on top of him, Brandon held him in a front choke hold arm bar.

"I'll make you pass out. You better tap out," warned Brandon.

With his neck stuck in his younger brother's tight headlock, Maleek's breath was quickly going away. He placed his palms flat on the ground, to the left and right side of Brandon's head. He then bear-crawled with his legs. His butt was sticking in the air. It looked like a yoga session. With all his strength, he sprung forward with his legs.

His body slowly did a front seesaw, causing him to land on his back. He broke loose from the frontal headlock. The two of them turned their heads inward. Lying on their backs, they locked eyes as they lay in opposite directions. Both hopped up. Maleek rose up quicker, though. Brandon tried to gain some distance by running forward. Maleek jumped on his back like he was a horse. "Yee-haw," yelled Maleek. He caught Brandon in a choke hold from behind. He also wrapped his legs around his hips, clinging on to him, bearing all his weight upon him.

He began spinning in circles, trying to get his older brother off his back. He fought hard like a bull in the rodeo. "Old McDonald had a farm. E-I-E-I-O," sung Maleek as he bronco-busted his brother's back. Brandon was slowly getting fatigued. He gradually fell to one knee.

"Get up, boy! Fight!" yelled Tyrone. Brandon stood back up, then continued to twirl in circles. Maleek tightened his choke hold. He started singing again.

"London bridge is fallin' down, fallin' down."

Brandon gently went back down to one knee. He slowly collapsed on the right side of his body.

"You better tap out or go night-night," foretold Maleek. A minute went by as he held his brother in the rear naked choke. Brandon refused to tap out; he started feeling the drowsiness. He began nodding to sleep. Finally, he tapped out. "Yeah!" shouted Maleek as he released Brandon and stood up to his feet. He placed his right foot on top of Brandon's chest while catching his breath. He pounded his chest like a gorilla. The rest of the family began walking into the house.

"Give me my money, you bootlicker," muttered Uncle Roy as he snatched the two hundred-dollar bills out of Tyrone's hand.

Brandon regained his wind. "Get your freaking foot off me. You notorious booty bandit," he shouted as he slapped Maleek's foot off him. He got to his feet with an angry stare. He glanced at Maleek, then walked toward the front door. Tyrone patted him on the back and walked inside the house with him. Maleek, Amy, Uncle Roy, and Tawanna all remained outside.

Chapter 7

Leg-Jacking

Maleek walked past Amy and Tawanna first. He imitated the posture of a gorilla, poking his elbows outward, hanging his forearms as low as his knees with his back bent over a little bit. He also walked bow-legged. "You think you so rough," said Tawanna.

He quickly turned around. "Huh! Huh!" snorted Maleek as he lifted his arms, sounding and acting like a gorilla.

"Ah!" screamed Tawanna as she burst off in a sprint, leaving Amy behind. Still mimicking a gorilla, he spun back around. He gave Amy a serious ape stare. He walked past her and snorted, looking funny.

As she started to blush, she covered her mouth with her hand. She hid her laughter as she smiled. *Wow, he's turning me on in a beastly way*, she thought in her head. "Boy! My nephew is a pure silverback," bragged Roy. He wrapped his arm around Maleek's shoulder. "Let's go eat, nephew." The two of them went through the front door. He gave Maleek the four hundred dollars.

Tawanna strolled back up close to Amy. She saw her face completely red from watching Maleek walk inside the house. "Girl! Don't let him impress you like that."

"He's so strong," replied Amy.

"Forget him, girl. Let's go eat." She led her best friend into the house. Everybody gathered in the kitchen to make their plates. There was one round table in the kitchen that accommodated four people.

Another square table was stationed in the dining room. It held twelve people. Shanna, Jojo, Anthony, and Nicole, the younger generation, all sat at the round table in the kitchen.

Granddad Willbe, Grandma Auatta, Momma D, and Aunt Abby all sat at the dining table first with their plates. Tyrone, Janeen, and Nat followed behind them to the table. Roy, Tawanna, Amy, and Becky sat down next. Only one seat was open. Brandon and Maleek were the only two still fixing their plates. Brandon noticed the only seat open. He hurried up and sat down in it.

After making his plate, Maleek went into the dining room. He looked at the table and saw that all the seats were taken. "Go eat in the living room. Don't spill nothing on my carpet neither, jailbird," said Momma D.

Maleek was feeling like an outsider. He looked down at the table and saw two turkey legs on his dad's plate. "Dad, are you going to eat both of those turkey legs?" he asked.

"No, I cut them off for me and my son Brandon," answered Tyrone. He then put one of the only two turkey legs on Brandon's plate. Granddad Willbe shook his head in discontent at what he was observing and hearing.

"Come on, nephew. We both can eat and watch TV in the living room. Let these circus misfits eat together," said Uncle Roy as he got out of his seat with his plate. Maleek turned about to follow his uncle.

"That's right! Go eat by yourself in solitary. Just like you did in prison, you loser," mumbled Brandon. *Poor Maleek*, thought Amy. Maleek changed directions, then moved toward his younger brother's back. Brandon sensed Maleek coming; he covered his head. Maleek reached over his shoulder and grabbed his turkey leg, then stepped back.

He bit a huge chunk off it. Brandon uncovered his head to find his turkey leg gone. He twisted his back to look over his shoulder. There stood his older brother eating his turkey leg like a lion stealing a hyena's meal. *Oh my*, thought Amy. Everyone sitting at the table had their mouths wide open in unbelief, surprised at what Maleek did. Brandon scooted his chair back to stand up.

"If you knew what's good for you, boy, you better stay in that chair!" said Maleek with meat stuffed in his mouth. He then walked off, laughing like an evil tyrant. Feeling sad and punked, Brandon looked down at his plate, ashamed to show his face to the family at the table. He sniffled a little bit.

"It's all right, baby," encouraged Becky as she rubbed him on the shoulder.

"That Negro done lost his mind," uttered Aunt Abby.

Chapter 8

Handful

"Boy! I'm going to beat the booty hairs off your ass," yelled Momma D. She slammed her napkin on the table, then scooted her chair back to stand up.

"You better leave that boy alone. Sit your whale blubber back in that chair before I break a two-by-four over your skull," shouted Granddad Willbe. Amy and Tawanna, as well as the rest of the family, covered their mouths, trying to hide the chuckling.

"Daddy!" she replied in dismay as she slowly sat back down in her seat.

"Daddy my ass! What'd I tell yo high-yellow ass about back talk? Now hush your chubby ass up so I can pray to the Lord for this lovely, delicious, scrumptious meal. Now everybody lock hands and bow your heads," he commanded. They all did as he ordered. After blessing the food, they ate dinner.

When he was done eating, Maleek changed back into his clothes. The time was 4:10 p.m. He had to be at work by 5:00 p.m. He hugged all his family members, then exited the front door. Amy tapped Tawanna on the shoulder, then winked at her. They both chased after Maleek through the front door. "Ha, big bro, will you help me out?" asked Tawanna.

For once she acknowledged him as a brother. Not just a brother, though, a big brother. He couldn't believe it; he finally felt respected. Delighted. "Sure! What is it, my sista?"

"Carry this suitcase inside for me and Amy."

"Where is it?"

"Follow me," insisted Amy. She walked in front of them, putting a little twitch in her hips. She popped the trunk to her car. "It's right there." She pointed. He easily lifted it. "Right this way. I need to open the front door." He shut the trunk. Amy led the two siblings to her front door. She slightly bent over and slowly placed the key in the lock.

"Dang, Amy, you got a big butt for a White girl," said Tawanna. Maleek glanced at her ass, then looked away.

"You're just being nice," she replied.

"No! For real. What do you think, Maleek?" By this time, Amy had led them inside her house. They all stood in the hallway.

"Hm! I wasn't looking," he lied.

"Don't hate because she's White. Just answer my question," said Tawanna.

"It's probably fake anyhow. White women are always getting plastic surgery or injections."

"You can spot the tell-tale signs that indicate a fake butt. Thighs don't match the hips or legs. A real butt is normally soft, firm, and jiggles moderately. Not all loose, like the lard on a fat person's triceps. See, look." Amy turned her back toward them. She pulled down her pants and bent over a little bit. She had a thong on.

Tawanna pinched her butt. "Oh yeah, that's 100 percent grade-A ass right there. Like a Nolan Ryan angus beef. Touch it, Maleek."

His eyes locked in on her voluptuous rear with his mouth wide open. He quickly wiped the drool off his bottom lip. "No, I better not," he responded.

"You remember when we were kids, Maleek? We always used to play hide-and-go-get-it. We've been friends forever. Just grab it so you know that it's real," Amy prompted. "I won't get mad." She was glancing over her shoulder while bending over. She smiled at him. "Go ahead."

He couldn't resist. He reached his hand out. He grasped it firmly. She let him massage it for about ten seconds. He snapped out of his attraction, pulling his hand back. "Okay, it's real. I must go now. I need to get to work." He scurried out the front door with an erection.

Amy pulled her pants up, then faced Tawanna. "Did you see that? I had him hypnotized. He likes me still."

"You right, girl. He's trying to stay steadfast on that pro-Black perspective. You got him wrapped around your finger like a ring-pop. He'll give in sooner or later. He hasn't had no pussy since leaving prison. Let's tell him happy Thanksgiving," said Tawanna.

Chapter 9

Black on Blue

Both came outside. "Happy Thanksgiving, Maleek," shouted Amy and Tawanna simultaneously.

Opening his door, he paused. Then he stared at them. "Tell that to the poor Native Americans who were suckered into accepting blankets with measles on them from the filthy Europeans who invented this phony-baloney holiday," he replied. Maleek hopped into his car, shutting the door behind him. He drove off on his way to Arlington.

"Prison really left an effect on him, but he's correct about Thanksgiving. The pilgrims had done some jacked-up shit," agreed Amy.

"Yeah, that nigga is fucked up in the head. He probably got rapped," guessed Tawanna as she and Amy watched him drive away.

The time now was 4:23 p.m. Maleek had his work outfit stored in his trunk. He drove to the end of Beltline Road. Just as he was about to get on Highway 183 heading west, about forty feet from the freeway entrance ramp, he spotted flashing lights in his rearview mirror.

A cop was pulling him over. "Fuck!" cursed Maleek. He pulled over and parked in the empty parking lot of the Irving Mall. Taking his time, the police officer nonchalantly marched up to his driver-side window then tapped on the glass. Maleek rolled down the window.

"You know why I'm pulling you over, Maleek?" asked the officer.

"Yeah, I know why. It's because I'm a young, handsome Black male, you racist, redneck, bigoted, doughnut-coffee-dipping, pig-slop-munching, buzz-haircut, testicle-grabbing, turkey-neck warthog. Can't stand the sight of a successful Black man," he answered.

"Wow! That was totally unexpected. How can I be racist if I'm Black? I haven't seen you since high school. I just wanted to chitchat with you," responded Jamal. The two of them had gone to MacArthur High School, and they both played on the same football team.

"I have nothing to say to you. I don't make small talk with piggy-boy sellouts."

"Well, fuck you too! Successful! Huh! What a joke, I should write you a ticket for this ragamuffin hoopty you are driving. Or should I smear it on your dusty-ass windows? It'll read, 'Maleek's clunker needs cleaning. Violation: not sanitary.'"

"Look, man! I need to go to work. How about you go back to your farm department and check in with your slave master, Old McDonald."

"Ha, man! It's not my fault you chose a life of crime. Now you're a nobody slash loser convict, stressed out on his menopause. It's probably the nightmares you have from getting your poop pushed in every night."

"Look here, Wilber, when you're done doing flips, helping Charlotte entertain the White man with her webs, saving your bacon, I need to get to work. You *comprende* me, or should I talk in Johnny Law language? Oink! Oink!" teased Maleek.

"Haha! That's real funny. I see it was a mistake even trying to talk with you. I heard you was on some pro-Black shit with your wannabe, fake-ass Marcus Garvey. Prison has fucked your head up. It was nice seeing you again, asshole. I'll let you go now. I know you got burgers to go and flip and catch grease on your shirt," said Jamal, as he slowly walked back to his squad car.

He poked his head out the window as he watched the cop walk away. "How in the hell do you know where I work at?" yelled Maleek.

"Every time I handcuff your sister to the bed rail then ram her ass from behind like a car derby, she tells me everything," he answered as he kept walking to his patrol car with his back to Maleek.

"Motherfucker!" he cursed. He started his engine and drove away, on his way to Arlington. "Goddammit, what is Tawanna thinking? Fucking Porky the Pig, telling him all my business." During the whole twenty-minute trip to Arlington, he cursed out loud to himself.

Chapter 10

Happy Ending

The time was 5:07 p.m. when he arrived at the parking lot of his job, Mr. Yumburger. After parking his car, he pulled his work clothes out of his trunk. He went inside the burger restaurant and made a beeline straight to the restroom. There were only two toilet stalls with doors. One had an "out of order" sign on it. A person had the other one occupied.

    He started removing his clothes. He stripped all the way down to his underwear. He began to fold up the clothes he had taken off. A squeaky noise was heard; it was the door of the toilet booth. Somebody was coming out of it. He spun around to see who it was.

    "Martha! What in the world are you doing in here?" asked Maleek. He quickly attempted to put his pants on. He crashed to the ground trying to do so. Martha was a coworker at Mr. Yumburger. She was a forty-three-year-old Mexican lady who couldn't read or understand English. He dropped his jeans as he fell to the dirty bathroom floor. She picked up the slacks, then waited for him to stand up. He stood up, then snatched the britches from her. He held them in his hand.

    "*Me conocer no inglés*," replied Martha.

    "I know you don't know any English. How many times do I have to explain to you? This is the men's bathroom. You're always using this restroom," he said while standing in his skivvies.

    "Me conocer no inglés."

"Ah!" He moaned in frustration as he placed his hand on his forehead. He pointed at the urinal. "Only men pee-pee in that." She kept eyeballing his body.

"Que?" she replied. He pointed at his penis, still in his undergarment, then pointed at the urinal.

"Only men. Pee-pee in that," he repeated. He kept pointing back and forth at his rod and the urinal, trying to make her understand.

She extended her arm, grabbing his balls. "*Si,*" she uttered, while cuffing his balls firmly.

"Huh!" he muttered. He was surprised that she seized his private part, making him flinch. He had been out of prison for three years. Besides Amy, this was the first time he had contact with a woman. His erection popped up like a slice of bread in a toaster. He clutched the wrist of her arm that she was holding his johnson with.

With her free hand, she grabbed the wrist of his arm that he was using to clutch her arm. "Huh!" he mumbled in shock, looking at her like she was crazy.

"No, no, *nino. Relájate, estás tenso y estresado. Déjame ayudarte a que te sientas mejor,*" explained Martha. Maleek couldn't speak Spanish very well. He could understand it, though. She had told him, "No, no, baby. Relax, you're tensed and stressed. Let me help you feel better."

With her hand held tight on his little man, he started pondering in his head, *She's right. Plus she's not bad-looking for a forty-three-year-old. I haven't been touched by a woman in three years. It feels so tantalizing.* He let go of her wrist, then rested his palms on her shoulders. Being from Mexico, she had never come across a Black man. She wanted to see if the African man had a big penis, a rumor she heard in Mexico. She was thrilled that Maleek accepted her pass.

In a rush, she pulled his underwear to his ankles, leaving him butt naked.

"*Bien agradable! Los mito, ella estar* real." With her mouth wide open in amazement, she'd said, *Good gracious! The myth, it be real.* She started stroking his penis. *I hope nobody walks through that door,* he thought. After six years of being abstinent from sex, which was forced upon him for three years, he went into a state of bliss as the hands of a woman caressed his male ego.

"Ah," he groaned loudly. She caused him to ejaculate on the restroom floor. He smiled from ear to ear from intense feeling. He pulled up his underwear, then quickly got dressed into his work apparel. He placed his index finger in front of his lips. "Shh! Keep this on the down low. Don't tell anyone."

"*Secreto. Si, si, nino.*" She understood what he was telling her. *Secret, yes, yes, baby,* she replied. She then pinched his cheekbone and shook his face a little bit. As she walked by him, she smacked him on the ass and laughed on her way out of the restroom. He took a deep breath and exhaled. *What just happened there?* he thought. He looked down at the floor and saw a large amount of semen. He scurried out of the restroom.

He went straight to the office. He punched in on the clock for work. The time was 5:19 p.m. "It took you long enough to get here," said J. "I thought I seen you walk in about ten minutes ago. Take these headphones and watch the drive-through. I need to use the restroom." J was a sixteen-year-old high school student. He worked part-time at Mr. Yumburger. Maleek took the headphones from him, then looked around the kitchen. Amanda was working the front register. Martha had control of the deep fryer. Larry, the manager, was positioned at the grill. "Larry!" shouted Maleek.

"Yo, what's up, bro?" replied Larry.

"I'm not your damn brother. Why haven't you put the gender signs on the restroom doors? You said you were going to do it yesterday."

Chapter 11

You Looking at Me?

"My bad, I forgot. Ha, have you seen Troy? I need to get a sack."

"That's why you forgot. You are smoking that shit too much. Troy's begging ass will be here soon, asking for a hookup."

"Nobody ever eats inside anyhow. No big deal with the bathrooms." Larry was twenty-three years old. He acted and smoked like a hippie. His father, the ex-manager of Mr. Yumburger, gave him the position, then retired. Larry was a cool boss, but he was unprofessional and unreliable. Also, Maleek didn't like the fact that a younger White man was his boss. He often must do his job and keep the burger joint intact.

J strolled back into the kitchen; he took the headset back from Maleek. "Who left behind a big spit wad in the middle of the floor? On my way out, I accidently stepped in it. There were no paper towels in the restroom. I used the last of the toilet paper." He grabbed some napkins, then leaned over and used the cabinet to maintain his balance. He lifted his left foot, bending it inward. He rested his left ankle on his right knee. "This is the stickiest spit I have ever seen. Whoever it was must be a cigarette smoker." The semen was clinging to his shoe, hanging low. "Son of a bitch could have at least spat in the sink or toilet."

"Why are you looking at me? I didn't do it," mumbled Maleek.

"Chill out, man, I didn't say it was you. You're just standing in the direction I'm looking at." A shiny glare hit Maleek in the eyes, temporarily blinding him.

"What'd I tell you about shining that damn sunlight reflection in my face with that fucking mirror, Larry! Quit playing before I whoop your hippie, acid-tongue-melting-taking ass," fussed Maleek.

"Dude, I don't even have a mirror in my hand," responded Larry, with his elbow covering his forehead. Maleek peeped under his wrist to see where the glare was coming from. It was Martha, her mouth filled with diamonds and gold. She was smiling because she knew where that semen on J's shoe came from.

"It's Martha's bling-bling," said Amanda, working the front cash register.

"Stop cheesing, Martha. Your glistening grill is blinding me," complained Maleek. She went back behind the grill and kept cooking.

"How can she afford all that bling-bling?" asked J. "She had to spend at least fifty thousand or more on that grill piece."

"Dude! Maybe she's a drug-dealing kingpin from Mexico. You know, like Griselda Blanco," joked Larry.

"You say the most dumbest shit I ever heard. Make sure you put them gender signs on the bathroom doors. Today! Just in case we do get some customers inside the diner. And Griselda Blanco is from Columbia, not Mexico, you dope," said Maleek.

"Please put them signs on the door. I'm tired of telling Martha to go in the other bathroom," explained J.

Maleek had a guilty look on his face. "Why you say that for?" he asked.

J stared at him. "If a customer does come in, I don't want Martha to be seen in the wrong restroom."

"Oh!"

"You all right, bro?"

"Yeah, of course. What made you ask that? Do I look nervous?"

"You've been acting a little strange." J looked back at the grill where Martha was working. "Nobody ordered any food. Why is she cooking? She's been grilling for the last ten minutes." All of a sudden, somebody walked into the dining room. He went right to the front desk, then stood by the cash register.

"May I take your order?" asked Amanda, winking her eye.

"Ah, ha, yeah, baby. Let me get a big butt double with large breast with pink nipples. Skip the soda and give me a vanilla milkshake," ordered Troy in a provocative voice.

"Hm! Boy, you are so silly."

"Where's Larry and Maleek at?" She hollered their names for him, then placed her mouth close to his ear.

"I get off at ten," whispered Amanda.

Maleek, Larry, and J all began heading to the front register. "Why you still trying to whisper? We know you and Troy be fooling around. You only mess with him because he got weed," claimed Maleek.

Amanda put her hand to Maleek's face. "Whatever, talk to the hand."

"What'd I tell you about messing with them White she-devils, Troy? Your jungle fever gone get you put in the slammer," predicted Maleek.

"Man! It isn't 1950 anymore. Everybody dates outside their race. You know, homie, whatever floats your boat," Troy replied.

"Well, don't forget we Black folks came over here on a boat."

Chapter 12

Blackmail

"Why you always got to be on that racist stuff?" asked Larry.

"Why does the White man continue to oppress the poor African? That's the question you should be asking."

"It's not a race thing, it's a class thing. Also, you know it was other warring African tribes who helped the slave traders capture other Blacks, right?" J assumed.

"Whoa, little brother. Whose side you on? I wouldn't be surprised if it was some of your ancestors who did that," responded Maleek.

"Ha, bro. I'm just speaking the truth and history. You're just mad because the truth hurts."

"Is that so. When Harriet Tubman was leading Blacks to the North, it was probably your great-grandfather's great-great-grandfather who was crying like a little sissy, whining about how he doesn't wanna run. 'The White man be good to me.' Harriet Tubman had to point a gun at his punk ass just to get him to run."

"I wouldn't be surprised if your great-granddaddy's great-great-granddaddy was so stupid, his dumb ass was still working on the plantation after the Civil War, looking at the Emancipation proclamation, then saying, 'Well, Anne May, we better get to picking that cotton. I don't know what that paper says. Besides, one day, I'm gone be a house nigga.'" J and Maleek stared at one another while everyone else was laughing.

"You must want me to kick yo little smart Black ass," suggested Maleek.

J raised his hands as if a cop had yelled *freeze*. "Ha, bro, you started the clowning first. I just fired back, man."

"Man, cuz! Leave that little nigga alone, man. You can't get mad at him because he knows more Black history than you," Troy stated.

Maleek glanced at Troy. "Quit using the *n* word, man! You're doing what the White man wants you to do."

"Actually, Black people choose to use that word themselves," J mentioned.

"Steve Urkel, I'm this close to knocking them glasses off your face," threatened Maleek.

"Screw this Black history lesson slash pro-Black shit. Somebody hook me up with some food," shouted Troy.

"What you in the mood for, Troy? I got you," assured Larry.

"My nigga," replied Troy as he put out his hand to give Larry some dap.

"Fo shizzle, my nigga!" responded Larry as he dapped hands with Troy.

"Larry! What'd I tell you about saying the *n* word?" griped Maleek.

"Hm!" mumbled Larry.

"Chill out, Huey Newton. He's talking to me. I gave him permission to say it," acknowledged Troy.

"How about I whoop your ass first, then his," responded Maleek.

"Man! Prison has fucked your head up, bro. What's kicking my ass going to accomplish?" pleaded Troy. "We supposed to be brothers."

"Yeah, Maleek, you've never been the same since you got out of prison," agreed Larry.

"Yeah, man, you need to get laid or something. Perhaps if you smoke some weed, it could help," suggested J.

Maleek looked at J. "What you know about smoking Mary Jane, youngsta?"

"Don't let these glasses fool you, Fredrick Douglass. I'm not a dork."

"Fredrick Douglass, huh! I should call yo momma and tell her you been smoking."

J gave Maleek a funny stare. "You can't do that. You don't even have my phone number."

"I do Larry's job. That means payroll, and stocking the supplies and equipment for the restaurant. Also, I do the work schedule. I got your home address and your house phone number."

"You're a convict, you wouldn't snitch. Would you?"

"He just pulling your chain, J. Maleek won't snitch," assured Troy. "Would you, Maleek?"

"I'm not calling the police, so it's not snitching. With that being said, if you ever insult my family bloodline again, I'll watch yo momma beat yo ass like my momma did me," told Maleek.

"But you made fun of me first," replied J.

"What can I say? It's a cold world. Say one more word, I'll dial your phone number right now."

"All right, I'm sorry. I won't say a word." With a sad look in his face, he looked down at the ground.

"Yeah, that's right, you little punk. You know what, you're dismissed." Maleek shooed J away with his hand as if he were a king telling a jester to go away. "Go clean them bathrooms," he demanded.

"But it's your job to clean tonight," argued J.

Maleek grabbed his cell phone out of his pocket, then put it to his ear. "What was that? I couldn't hear you. Did you say something? Is this J's mother I'm speaking with?"

"Okay, just put the phone away. I'm on my way to clean the restrooms now." J quickly started making his way to the bathrooms. "Punk bitch," he mumbled under his breath.

"That's blackmail. You wrong for that," said Amanda.

"Make sure you get that spit wad off the floor too," shouted Maleek. Martha poked her head around the grill and started laughing.

"What's she laughing for?" wondered Larry. Grinning, Martha displayed her iced-out grill, causing a glare.

"Quit cheesing, Martha, you are blinding us with your bling," shouted Maleek. She positioned her head back behind the stove.

"She sure has been happy today," observed Amanda.

Maleek gave Amanda a guilty look. "Why are you looking at me like that?" he asked while shrugging his shoulders. "Why the hell is she still cooking? We haven't had any customers for the past forty minutes."

"She probably has a household full of relatives. You know them Mexicans be having ten to twelve people all bunched up. Just to save money, all of them pay a small percent for the rent," stereotyped Larry.

"*Estupido galleta, tu mama es una perra.*" *You stupid cracker, your mama be a slut*, said Martha in Spanish.

Chapter 13

I'm the Boss

"I swear she knows English. What did she say, Maleek?" asked Larry.

Maleek laughed. "Nothing, don't worry about it."

"What's up, man? May I get some food or what?" asked Troy.

"What you want to eat?" asked Larry. Troy stared at the menu even though he knew it by heart.

"Let me get a number 2, supersized," answered Troy. Larry joined Martha on the stove. He began cooking Troy's meal. Seven minutes later, he sacked the food up, then headed toward the front register. He set the sack on the cabinet. As Troy went to pick it up, Maleek quickly snatched it away from him.

"What's up with you, fool?" blurted Troy.

"Let me see a dub sack," replied Maleek. Troy pulled a weed bag out of his pocket and gave it to him. "Yeah, this sack is fat. About time. Here," he said as he threw money on the cabinet.

Troy picked it up. "This is only twelve dollars."

"Your meal cost seven dollars. Now we're even."

"Aw! That's messed up. What about the extra dollar?"

Maleek placed the weed sack in his pocket. "I'll be using that dollar to help with the cigars."

"You have a dime bag on you, bro?" Larry asked.

Troy grabbed a dime sack out of his back pocket. "Here you go, Larry." He tossed the weed sack to him.

45

Larry observed the weed sack he had just received. "Sweet, this is a fat sack." He reached into his pants pocket, pulled out a ten-dollar bill, then handed it to Troy.

"I'm out of here, y'all. I'll holla at y'all later."

"I'll call you, Troy, once I get off work," said Amanda. He waved bye to her as he exited Mr. Yumburger. The time now was 6:09 p.m. On a Thanksgiving, Thursday. No customers came to Mr. Yumburger because of Thanksgiving. Time seemed to be going by slow to them. The five of them were scattered around the dining room, lounging around in chairs.

"We been here all day and no customers. Would it be okay if I get off early, Larry?" asked J.

"Larry may have the title of boss, but you know who's running the show," reminded Maleek. "It's 8:40 p.m. You get off at 10:00 p.m. Go ahead, little brother, go home." J ran to the clock and punched out. Then he ran toward the exit door. He came to a standstill and turned around.

He had a smile on his face. "Thanks, Maleek," shouted J. He then walked out the burger joint.

"Lock all the doors, Larry," demanded Maleek.

Larry glanced at him. "It's not ten o'clock yet."

"Ain't nobody coming in here to eat. Just lock the doors, O-Pee."

Larry followed Maleek's order. Maleek cut on the radio, then cranked the volume up. Next, he pulled out his weed sack, then began breaking the marijuana down.

Chapter 14

High on the Job

"How you plan on smoking that?" wondered Amanda. He pulled a cigar out of his shirt pocket.

Larry came close to Maleek and Amanda and sat beside him. "All this damn seating space, yet you have to sit your pale ass right next to me. Quit crowding me, scoot the hell over," griped Maleek.

"Oh! My bad, dude. I got excited when I seen the green," replied Larry. He stood up, then sat across the table from his coworker. He finished removing all the seeds and stems from the dope. He grabbed his pocketknife to split open the cigar. His cell phone started ringing. "You want me to roll the blunt up while you talk on the phone?"

"You're not going to break the only cigar we got. Your jive ass can't even roll up a joint without tearing it."

"Don't touch it, Larry. Let me roll that shit up," Amanda insisted. Maleek went to the restroom to answer his phone. The music was too loud for him.

Chapter 15

Party Invitation

"Hello," said Maleek as he answered his phone.

"What time you get off work?" asked Tawanna over the phone.

"At 12:00 p.m. Why, what's up?" he replied.

"There's a party at eleven o'clock. I just wanted to let you know," she answered.

"Since when do you tell me about events happening? What are you up to?" he suspiciously asked.

"Oh, hush up, boy! I just thought that you would want to come. This party is going to be the bomb! Write this address down." While Tawanna announced the address, he wrote it down. "Everyone must pitch in on the drinks. So buy beer or some alcohol. Oh yeah! You don't get off until twelve. It'll be too late for you to purchase any drinks."

"I can get off early," assured Maleek.

"Okay, cool. Where can we find weed? Do you know anybody that will deliver? Damn near everyone coming to this party smokes."

"I'll bring Troy with me to the party."

"All right, sounds like a plan to me. See you then, bye."

To keep her from hanging up the phone, he shouted "Wait."

"What? I'm still here," she responded.

"I know you eat pork, but I didn't know you like to lay in the bed with it."

Tawanna had a vision of herself lying in bed with strips of bacon. "What are you talking about?"

"I suppose you gave some ass just to have a get-out-of-jail-free pass."

"Oh! You're talking about Jamal. Haha! Very funny."

"Did you lure him in with some coffee and doughnuts?"

"You know what, Negro, you can kiss my Black ass. That's my business. How you know about us anyways?"

"Your ticket-writing, butt-gripping piggy boyfriend pulled me over to have a chat. We had an argument, he got angry, then threw it in my face that he's banging my sister like a bumper car. If you like selling out to a cop, fine and dandy. That's your business. But don't be telling that jabroney anything about me," demanded Maleek.

"Boy! Please, you ain't got no business. You are flipping burgers."

"Whatever. If you expect me to mind my business, quit telling Alonzo about mine."

"Alonzo! Who is that?" she wondered.

"You ain't never seen the movie *Training Day*?"

She had to think for a second. "Fuck you, nigga, bye," shouted Tawanna as she hung up the phone.

"Will Maleek be at the party?" asked Amy.

Tawanna glanced at her best friend. "Yeah, he'll be there. Oh! Girl, he makes me so damn mad. He always got some slick-ass shit coming out his mouth."

"It's a defense mechanism."

"Defense mechanism! What do you mean?"

"This is a tactic that I learned from patients I treated in the past while attaining my master's degree in psychology. Maleek feels that he is regarded as less than a man. He doesn't feel respected. He releases his anger with cynical insults. In reality, he himself is bitter. Without knowing how to express himself, he holds his anger inside. He needs someone to talk with. Once I get ahold of him, he'll change his perspective."

"I'd be upset too if I was flipping burgers."

"Stop being so mean, Tawanna. You promised me that you would be nice to him."

"I'm trying, Amy, but you didn't hear what he just said to me on the phone. He also suspected that I was up to something, but he doesn't know that you'll be at the party."

Amy went to her closet and opened the doors. She grabbed two dresses and held them in front of her. "Which one should I wear? The red or blue?"

"Maleek's favorite color is blue."

"Blue! It used to be red when he was younger."

"I guess when he went to prison, he got the blues," joked Tawanna.

Amy placed her left hand on her left hip and leaned to the right. "Tawanna!"

"All right, I'll quit the jokes. I hope you can persuade him to do the same."

"You remember when you called him big bro?"

"Yeah, you're talking about when I asked him to carry your luggage inside," answered Tawanna.

"Exactly, you used reverse psychology. Without even knowing it. He smiled when he heard you say that. It's not hard to earn his respect. Treat him like what he is to you, an older brother."

"I can do that. What about his racist attitude toward White people? How will you deal with it?"

"Maleek is not racist. He just went to prison and seen another side of life. I'm going to be truthful with you, Tawanna. Black people have a right to be resentful toward White people."

"Why would that be the case?" she wondered.

Amy took a deep breath as she got ready to explain her theory. "We all know about slavery. In schools across America, society makes it seem like Abraham Lincoln started the Civil War to free the slaves. In actuality, he only made that move to slow down the South's income. Lincoln was convinced by Fredrick Douglass to allow the free slaves to fight in the Civil War. Even though the North needed Blacks to win the war, the White man's pride almost didn't allow it."

"Please, Amy, just stop. This is the future, not the past."

"I know, but it needs to be told why Maleek feels the way he does. He learned more about Black history in probably just a month within prison than he did in elementary all the way through high school. America is scared to teach the whole truth about its ugly past. It's also evident that more Black males are incarcerated more than any other race. Did you know there are more White drug dealers than Black? And the White population is significantly larger than the Black population. Yet Black males are targeted more. Not to mention the unemployment rate of Blacks, which is double the entire population."

"It's all about a person's decision and choices they make in life. Blacks need to stop blaming the White man," argued Tawanna.

"To be honest with you, a lot of people don't have those choices. Nor the resources to move out of their situation. To top it off, not everyone is meant to go to college. Not everyone has the brain smarts. If they can't find a job, then what?"

Tawanna took a deep breath. "I suppose you're right. Let's go get ready for this party, girl." They began to freshen up for the party.

Meanwhile, at Mr. Yumburger, Amanda had just completed rolling up a huge cigar full of weed. Maleek, Larry, and Martha were cleaning up the restaurant. Maleek told them that they would all get off early today. As soon as they smoked the blunt. He also called Troy, telling him to get ready for the party. The time now was 9:03 p.m. Maleek figured he'd close Mr. Yumburger at 10:00 p.m., leaving him an hour to get ready for the party.

Chapter 16

Battle Stations

Just as Amanda was about to spark the blunt, "Hello, anyone here?" asked some unknown person in the dive-through speaker.

"I can't believe somebody showed up during Thanksgiving. Everybody to their stations," yelled Maleek. He sounded like a captain on a battleship, demanding all his sailors at their battle stations. All four of them took off sprinting toward the kitchen. Maleek was headed for the register window. While running, he snatched up the headphones to answer the drive-through. Amanda bolted to the deep fryer. Both Martha and Larry were going to the grill.

"Huh! *Mi, mi, me duele*," uttered Martha as she lost her balance and fell to the ground. *My, my, my, that hurt*, she blurted. Larry turned around. *Man down*, he thought. He reached down to help her get up. She slapped his hand away. "*Llegale, gvero, tu lo tienes que hacer.*" *Go, White boy, you must do it*, she said. Larry had no clue what she said, but he took off running.

Martha lay on the ground, holding her chin.

"Hello, is this place open?" asked the mysterious person speaking in the drive-through speaker.

Maleek made it to the drive-through window. "Thank you for choosing Mr. Yumburger. May I take your order?" By this time, Martha slowly limped to the grill and stood next to Larry. With the blunt tucked in her shirt pocket, Amanda stood next to the deep fryer. All three of them could hear the customer over the loudspeaker, waiting to hear the order.

"Yes, let me have a number 3 and a number 1. I would like both meals Mr. Yum-sized."

"You got it. Will that be it for you, sir?"

"Yes, that'll be it," replied the customer.

"Your total is $19.43. Please drive up to the window." As Maleek waited for the customer, everyone else was preparing the meals. A nice-looking luxury car pulled up to the window. He opened the drive-through window. "Your total is $19.43," Maleek said. The guy handed him a twenty-dollar bill. Maleek placed the Jefferson bill in the register, then gathered up the change and gave it to the customer.

While he was retrieving his change, the man asked, "Maleek, is that you?"

Maleek looked closely at his face. "Brad," he replied.

"Yeah, it's me, Brad. From MacArthur. We ran track together. How have you been, man? It's great to see you, bro. I haven't seen you since high school," he said excitedly.

"Well, despite being Black in a White man's world, I'm still alive. Don't call me bro, you're White."

With an appalled look on his face, Brad thought he was just joking around. He smiled, then continued to chat with his long-lost friend. "Ha! You remember that girl Tinna you hooked me up with in high school?"

"Yeah, you're speaking of Black Tinna. She was on the girls' track team."

"Thanks to you, Maleek, we're married. I was too shy to approach her, but you intervened. Without you, my marriage would've never happened. We've been together since then. After all these years I've been wanting to thank you so much. Tinna also." Someone leaned over the armrest from the passenger seat, showing her face.

"Hi, Maleek. Thank God for your good spirit and what you did. Good to see you again," Tinna greeted as she waved at him.

Maleek bagged their food up and handed it to them. "Well, the White man doesn't need slavery anymore to get some Black ass," he spoke.

"What did he say?" asked Tinna.

"Haha!" laughed Brad. "He's just playing around. A little harsh, but funny."

"Why are you two eating fast food during Thanksgiving?" asked Maleek.

"Both of our families went out of town," answered Brad.

"I see you got a sista that can't cook soul food," mumbled Maleek.

Tinna had her mouth wide open, amazed at what she had just heard. "I don't think he's playing around," she determined.

Brad glanced at her, then Maleek. "Oh! He's just wisecracking, like back in the days. Right, old buddy?"

With a serious facial expression, disapproval showed in Maleek's face. His big, long lips were shaped in the form of a rainbow, similar to a clown appearing to be sad. His upper lip was tucked in as his bottom lip stuck out further. This look had become his signature look. Between the three of them, they gazed at one another. The moment of silence was awkward. "Does it look like I'm playing, Willie Lynch?" replied Maleek.

Brad couldn't believe what he was hearing. "Willie Lynch! Come on, man! You know me."

Tinna tapped her husband on the leg. "Let's go, honey. He's not the same Maleek we used to know." Brad had a dispirited look on his face as he slowly drove off, wondering what was wrong with his old friend.

"Let's smoke this blunt," insisted Maleek as he spun around. Amanda, Larry, and Martha all had their arms crossed, displaying their disappointment on how he treated his old friends.

"What's wrong with you?" asked Amanda.

"You need to visit a psychologist," recommended Larry.

"I don't need to do nothing, Dr. Phil. All you need to do is spark that blunt up, Iggy Azalea. Hell! When this government pays reparations, then I'll see a psychologist."

"Whatever," replied Amanda.

"Why you got your arms crossed, Martha? You can't even speak English," said Maleek. The time now was 9:20 p.m. It took them thirty minutes to finish smoking. The four of them began to shut down Mr. Yumburger. As they exited the restaurant, Martha was carrying nine bags of food. Maleek and Larry both had a set of keys to the burger joint. The two of them were the last to walk out of the building.

"My goodness, Martha! Do you need a shopping cart for all those bags?" asked Larry.

"*No, panocha. Necesito que no te precupes de mireconocer oficio.*"

No, you pussy. I need you to mind your own business, responded Martha.

"What did she say, Maleek?" asked Larry.

Maleek giggled. "She asked if you could help her carry some of those bags to her car."

"Sure, why not." Larry began to approach Martha. He tried to grab a few bags from her. She safeguarded her bags by putting them behind her back, withstanding his help.

She had a mean mug on her face. "Suplente, puto." *Back up bitch*, cursed Martha.

"Did she just call me a bitch?" asked Larry. "I can understand some curse words in Spanish. Huh!" he yelped in pain as Martha kneed him in the balls. He slowly fell to the ground while holding his nuts. Martha hopped in her car and drove off. "I may not have no kids because of you, Maleek," he shouted while lying on the ground.

"You're wrong for that," said Amanda as she and Maleek walked toward their apartment.

Chapter 17

History Lesson

"He'll be all right, but I probably won't," predicted Maleek.

"Why you say that? You okay?"

"The police will see me walking down the street with a White woman at night, then come and beat me up. So if you don't mind, please stand still and count to a hundred. Then continue walking."

"Shut up, you idiot, and keep walking. Besides, you're not leaving me out here alone. Your apartment is further past mine anyhow. I'm going to laugh at you one of these days when you fall in love with a White chick. Then what?"

"That'll never happen. I love my Black women."

"What if God intended you to fall in love with a certain woman? It just so happens that this lady is White. Or what if it's hard for you to find a Black woman that will accept you? What if a White lady overwhelms you with her love?" speculated Amanda.

Maleek gazed at her while he deeply thought about the question. "I doubt that would ever happen. You know why?"

"Why?" she responded.

"Because I'll never sell out."

"You're not selling out just because you date another race. Love is love," she debated. By this time, they had made it to Amanda's apartment. They came to a standstill.

"What do you know about love?" he asked.

Amanda slowly walked to her front door and opened it. Pausing in the middle of the doorway, she turned around to face Maleek. "I know once Cupid hits you with an arrow, you can't resist love."

"What the hell! Cupid! You can't be serious. You don't believe in a naked midget, or a baby flying around with a bow and arrow, do you?" he wondered.

"I'm not saying Cupid is real. I'm just speaking of love. Hm! You know. Hm! Like Valentine's Day," she muttered in a hesitant, unsure tone of voice.

Maleek rested his hands on his hips as he gave her an inexcusable stare. "Another fake holiday made up by the White man. Do you even know where that holiday is derived from? Huh! Well, do you?"

"Hm! It's were they pass out flowers, chocolates, and cards. From lover to…huh!" He interrupted her.

"Hush your feeble talk," shouted Maleek as he stopped her from rambling. "Till this day historians don't even know how Valentine's Day came about. My theory is I think it came from two martyrs of the early Christian church who had the name Valentine, who both happened to be saints. There are many stories. One story says that the Roman Emperor Claudius II in the AD 200s outlawed young men to be married. He thought that single men made better soldiers. A priest named Valentine disobeyed Claudius. Valentine was secretly marrying young couples.

"Once the Emperor found out, it's said that Valentine was beheaded on February 14, about AD 269. I don't know how true that is. There are many other stories."

"Oh!" she mumbled.

"Hell of a holiday, isn't it? Two men get their heads chopped off. Now everybody wants to pass out cards and chocolates."

"Why must you always take things out of context? Oh, you make me so angry," shouted Amanda. She slammed her front door.

"You're just mad because the truth hurts. Know your facts before you open them dragon lips of yours," shouted Maleek as he kept walking toward his apartment.

The time was now 10:09 p.m. Maleek got inside his apartment. He turned on some music, then began ironing his clothes. Romme woke up, yawning. He opened his room door to see what his roommate was up to.

"What are you doing?" asked Romme.

"Why you sleep all day during the day then stay up all night like a fucking leech-sucking vampire? That's the question you should be asking."

"Man! You know I work at night. Why you buggin'?"

"I'm going to a party. I'm leaving at 11:00 p.m. If you're going, I suggest you take a shower and brush your fangs," suggested Maleek. Romme closed his room door; he began getting ready for the party.

Maleek grabbed his cell phone; he dialed Troy's cell number.

"Hello," blurted Troy as he answered his phone.

"There's a party at 11:00 p.m. in Irving, you riding?"

"If I do, I'm bringing Amanda with me."

"That's cool. There's a lot of customers. You may want to bring a lot of weed."

"Already, baby! My clientele is going to hit the roof."

"Yeah, thanks to me, you chump. You owe me a twenty sack," Maleek claimed.

"What! You are taxing me. You're as bad as the government taxing medical weed. I got you, though. You driving?"

"Hell naw, fool, you driving. I'm not taking my Pinto up to the party just to be the laughingstock of the year. Besides, you gone be carrying a pound on you. Ride dirty in your own damn car. Be ready by 10:50 p.m. Swing by my apartment and pick me and Romme up."

"Foshow, cuz! I'll be there by ten fifty," assured Troy. The two of them hung up their cell phones. The time now was 10:10 p.m. Maleek finished ironing his clothes, then hopped in the shower. After cleaning his body, he brushed his teeth and got dressed. The time now was 10:45 p.m. Romme was waiting in the living room for Maleek. Freshly dressed, the two of them exited the apartment. Just as the front door was locked behind them, Troy pulled up in front of their apartment with Amanda in the front passenger seat. He was driving a four-door Tahoe, sitting on some twenty-four-inch spinners. Paint job was baby-blue candy paint. Tinted windows were halfway rolled down. His radio system was playing loudly.

Maleek and Romme jumped in the back seat.

Chapter 18

Numbskulls

The four of them began their trip to Irving. Maleek had always seen this vehicle in the parking lot of his apartment complex. Yet he never knew who owned it. He was sitting right behind the driver seat, to the rear of Troy. The music was so loud, other cars on the highway couldn't be heard. Maleek poked his head in between the passenger and driver seat. "I didn't know this was your ride!" he shouted.

Troy really couldn't hear him well. "You didn't know I was high! Is that what you said?" yelled Troy.

Maleek really couldn't understand him clearly. "I'm high. Amanda told you I got high earlier today," screamed Maleek.

"I didn't know you're a dike. No man told me anything earlier today," he shouted.

"You didn't know Amanda was a dike? She told your earlier today?" Maleek yelled.

"Let me get this correct. You're gay, and Amanda's a dike," Troy screamed.

Amanda turned down the volume to the radio. "You numbskulls, talk without the music blasting. Duh!"

While peeping in his rearview mirror, Troy had an unsettled look on his face. "Maleek, I didn't know you prefer sausages instead of fish," he pointed out in a subtle way.

"I like both. It depends on the time of day and what I'm in the mood for," replied Maleek.

"Was prison the cause for your change of desire?"

"No, I always liked both," he answered.

"Since we were kids! Wow! I never would've guessed that. Which one were you in prison? The sausage or the fish? Were you the pumper, or were you getting pushed in?"

Maleek looked at Troy like he was crazy. "What in the picnic basket are you talking about?"

"Look, man! We're friends and all, but I don't play them games. You won't try to take my buns, will you?" asked Troy.

"You're not a man rapist, are you, Maleek?" worried Romme.

"Why in the world would y'all assume that?" questioned Maleek.

Amanda had a grin on her face. "You big dummies! Just hush! The first question Maleek asked you was about your automobile! You thought he said something else because the music was playing loudly!"

"Oh!" responded Troy with a bewildered look on his face. "What was your question, Maleek?"

"I said that I didn't know this was your ride," answered Maleek. Troy was about to open his mouth to speak. "Just shut up, I can't believe you thought that I was gay." *Wham!* He slapped Troy on the back of his head. "Give me my twenty sack, fool." Troy tossed the sack over his shoulder. "If I was gay, I'd be the one taking the ass, not giving it," he said while stuffing the sack in his pocket.

Chapter 19

Finger Discount

"Yuck!" mumbled Amanda. "The way you be acting. It wouldn't surprise me if you went poop diving before. You haven't been with a woman since you've gotten out of prison."

"How you know what I've done? Are you a private investigator or something? You can't work for cheaters because I'm single," replied Maleek.

"Whatever," she responded. By this time, they were entering Irving city limits.

"Stop by the liquor store before you head to the party, Troy. I need to buy some beer and cigars," said Maleek. The time now was 11:05 p.m. They were only a few miles from the party. Troy, followed by Maleek, jumped out of the Tahoe. Troy covered his butt with his hands, then scooted to his left to allow Maleek to pass him. "What are you doing, man? Don't nobody want your hairy ass. I told you that I'm not gay." In unbelief, Maleek shook his head side to side, then passed Troy up and went inside the store.

Troy came in behind him. "Look, Maleek! Isn't that Nia right there by the soft drinks?" he said while pointing.

"Yeah, that is her," he confirmed.

"That girl was crazy about you in high school." Nia was one of the finest Black chicks in high school. She had a crush on Maleek in the past, only because he was popular. She was also the cousin of Jamal, the cop.

"Watch carefully, Troy. You might learn something, son." Maleek brushed his shoulders off, showing off. He then began to approach Nia. He slowly marched with a limp.

With her sight on the drinks, Nia didn't see Maleek to her left. Standing in front of the refrigerator door she was holding open, he took his index finger and began to smear in "ha baby" on the glass door. She looked at the words. Grabbed a twelve-pack of beer, she shut the glass door.

Squinting her eyes, she quickly recognized him. "Is that you, Maleek?" asked Nia.

"Yes, it is. I see you still looking good, baby. How about you give me your cell number? That way, we can rekindle our fire," sweet-talked Maleek.

"Boy, please!" she responded.

"Boy! I'm a grown-ass man. What's up with the attitude?"

"Look, don't get me wrong. I liked you in high school, and I'll admit you still fine looking, but I don't want no broke-ass jailbird. So the only fire you need to ignite is that one under the stove you are flipping burgers on."

"Damn! It's like that. You're a forty-niner fan, a gold digger, huh! How you know where I been and worked at anyhow?"

Nia started to walk away, then stopped in the middle of the aisle. "You must have forgot that Jamal is my cousin. It's fucked up how you treated him. So yeah, nigga, it's like that." She began to walk away again.

"That's why I didn't give you any play in high school anyways. Your attitude is like your breath in the past, funky," he yelled.

"Whatever, grill master!" yelled Nia as she continued to walk toward the cash register. *Forget her*, Maleek thought in his head. He grabbed a twenty-four-pack of beer. He made his way toward the cashier. He stood in line, behind Nia. He gazed up and down her body from behind.

"Damn, girl, you lost all your ass. You been sniffing cocaine?" asked Maleek. *Wham!* Nia spun around quickly, slapping him across the face. To his surprise, the clerk behind the cabinet covered his mouth.

63

Troy also covered his mouth. With his free arm, he pointed at Maleek while laughing. "Damn! She slapped the Black off yo face," he shouted.

Maleek held his right cheek while Nia purchased her twelve-pack of beer. The store attendant bagged the soft drinks and handed it to her. She turned around to leave, but she paused, then flinched at Maleek; he jumped and covered his face. "You better jump, you little bitch," cursed Nia. She greeted Troy as she walked by him. As she exited the convenience store, she flipped the middle finger.

Troy was giggling hard. "I learned something all right. I learned how not to get smacked."

Maleek stared at him while buying the twenty-four-pack of beers. He also bought a pack of cigars. "Man! Fuck you," he replied. He lifted the case of brew by its handle. He headed for the exit doors with the pack of cigars in his pocket. Troy opened the door for him. "Keep this to yourself," demanded Maleek.

"Don't worry, homie. Your diss is safe with me."

The two of them hopped in the Tahoe. "I saw Nia come out the store. Did you recognize her?" asked Romme.

"Man! Fuck Nia," answered Maleek. Troy snickered.

"What'd did she do to you?" asked Amanda.

"What are you? A reporter or something? Quit asking all of them damn questions, Barbara Walters," said Maleek.

"I was just wondering why you would curse her like that," she responded.

"All of them journalists going to the Middle East were also curious to report in the Middle East. Do you know what curiosity got them? Huh? Well, do you?"

Amanda looked confused. "News, I guess."

"No! They got their freakin' heads chopped off. That's the problem with you White folks. Y'all don't know how to mind y'all's own business."

"Why must you always refer to race? Who are you, Spike Lee or something?" she responded.

Troy began to drive off.

"I'm done answering questions. Turn up the music," ordered Maleek. Troy cranked up the volume as the four of them were on the way to the party. The time now was 11:15 p.m. They were not very far away from the party. About seven minutes later, the four of them arrived at their destination. Troy parked next to the curb. Nia had just finished parking her car. She exited her vehicle parked in front of Troy's Tahoe.

As Nia walked toward the house party, the four of them watched her while looking at the house simultaneously. "Whoa! This house is fully packed to capacity," said Romme. People were dancing and socializing in the front yard. The loud music could be heard outside. All four of them hopped out of the Tahoe and headed for the house.

"At what time should we leave the party?" asked Troy.

"I know you wanna sell your weed all night. We can be the last ones to leave. Hell, I don't care. I tell you what, I'll call your cell when it's time to go," replied Maleek.

Troy dapped hands with him. "Foshow, homie. Me and Amanda will see y'all around." Troy and Amanda separated from Maleek and Romme as they went into the midst of the crowd.

"Let's go inside, Romme. I need to put these beers on ice," said Maleek. The two of them made their way inside the packed-house party. People were bumping and grinding closely as they danced. The party was filled with old high school buddies.

"Maleek! Over here," shouted Tawanna from the kitchen. He and Romme made their way through the crowded living room into the kitchen. Amy and Jake were also in the kitchen. Jake was an old high school buddy of Maleek. They had run track together.

"Maleek and Romme. What's happening, my brothers?" asked Jake. He gave both of them a tight, friendly hug.

"What's good with you, man! Who told you about the party?" asked Maleek.

Chapter 20

Hidden Closet

"I'm hosting the party. This is my house," he answered.

"Man! That's great. It's good to see another Black man prosper."

Tawanna rolled her eyes at her brother. "Please, Maleek, no pro-Black shit tonight. We trying to get fucked up! Ha, Romme, I haven't seen you in a good grip. Give me a hug, boy." The two of them hugged.

"Ha, Romme," greeted Amy. She also gave him a hug. "What's up, Maleek? I like your outfit." She then hugged him tightly but didn't let go of him. When she unwrapped her arms from above his shoulders, she rewrapped them around his waist as she continued to talk, causing them to closely cuddle. "When Jake heard I was in town, he wanted to throw a party for my homecoming," she said, looking at Jake.

"Hm! Where's your icebox at? I need to put these beers on ice," said Maleek. With one hand, he gently unwrapped Amy's arms from around him. Jake led him to the cooler. He emptied half of the beer case into the cooler, the other half into the freezer.

"Man! Did you see Amy? She's smoking hot," said Romme.

"Of course I've seen her. She's only about ten yards away from us. Quit talking so loudly, she'll hear us, you fool."

Romme started to whisper in Maleek's ear. "Amy's staring at you hard. She had her eyes on you since we came in the kitchen. She likes you, Maleek."

Jake was surveying Maleek. "I can understand why she likes you. Look at you, man, you're in shape. You're fit," he said as he patted Maleek on the shoulder. Romme spotted a rainbow on his arm.

"Aw! Thanks, man. Can you tell that I've been hitting the iron? That's all I've been doing for the past few years in prison," said Maleek.

"Most definitely." He rubbed Maleek on the arm. "Your biceps and triceps are curved and ripped. Your chest is sticking out, even through your shirt. Your shoulders are up to your neck. You got it going on, bro," complimented Jake.

Maleek gave him a hug. "Thanks, man! I missed you, brotha."

"Well! Don't let me hold you two good-looking guys captive. Go have fun." Jake walked off, leaving them alone.

"Ha, man! I think Jake is gay. I saw a rainbow tattooed on his arm," said Romme.

"Stop it! He's the first person to treat me like a human being since I've been out of prison. Besides, you know Lucky Charms was his favorite cereal. He used to bring a box of Lucky Charms cereal to school every day. He never ate no school breakfast or solid food in the morning. He always ate Lucky Charms," claimed Maleek.

"I don't know, man. Maybe the Lucky Charms are just a front." Romme looked at the refrigerator. On top of the icebox were several boxes of Lucky Charms cereal. "You see, he still loves that same cereal. Plus, I could have sworn that Jake touched my butt when he hugged me."

Ten feet away, Amy was still staring at Maleek as she and Tawanna stood in the same spot. "Has he figured out that Jake is gay yet?" asked Amy.

"I doubt it. He wouldn't have given him a hug," Tawanna replied.

"What's up, man? Are you going to get at Amy or what?" asked Romme.

"You know I don't mess with snowflakes. You talk to her," Maleek responded.

"She likes you, not me. You are tripping, fool." Romme grabbed a shot glass off the cabinet, then chugged it. "Besides, that ain't no snowflake. She's a snow woman with some very nice size snowballs. If you know what I mean. I would love to stick my carrot inside her snow buns. I'm going to the dance floor. I'll see you around." He filled his shot glass back up with alcohol, then headed toward the living room. Maleek tried to follow him. Before he could, Tawanna shouted.

"Maleek! Hand me and Amy a shot glass." He stopped trailing Romme. He grabbed two shot glasses, then brought them over to Amy and Tawanna.

"Where's your drink at, Maleek?" asked Amy.

"Oh yeah! How rude of me." Maleek got him a shot glass also.

"On three, let's slam them, y'all," said Amy. She slowly counted to three. All three of them quickly downed their shots. "Woo!" yelled Amy. She then handed Maleek her keys.

"Why you give me your keys for?" he asked.

"You're my designated driver," she replied.

Tawanna grabbed Amy by the hand. "Come on, girl, let's go shake some ass." They both walked off.

"How y'all just gone make me a designated driver without asking?" shouted Maleek. They kept moving as they ignored him. "Ha, Salt 'n' Pepper, I know y'all hear me talking to you two." Not knowing what to do. He took a deep breath, then placed Amy's car keys in his pocket. He proceeded to the living room. It was crowded just like a nightclub.

Maleek slowly started moving through the packed dance floor. It was so crammed, he had to wiggle like a worm as he pressed through the swarm of partygoers. He was on his way toward Amy and Tawanna. As he made it within seven yards of them two, he saw Troy and Amanda greeting Amy and Tawanna. "Huh!" mumbled Maleek as he jumped. He quickly turned around to look behind him. Somebody had pinched him on the butt.

Three men and one woman was directly behind him. Two of the men were dancing together. The third man was dancing with the woman. He had no clue who pinched his ass. With a look of disgust on his face, he kept moving. As he got closer to where he was headed, he saw Tawanna whispering in Troy's ear. When she was done talking, Troy walked away with Amanda trailing him. They disappeared within the middle of the crowd.

He sealed off the distance between him, Amy, and Tawanna. Then began ranting while they were dancing. "I can't be a designated driver for you two. I rode here with Troy."

"Don't worry about me. I'm going to call Jamal for my ride," replied Tawanna.

"Will he make you take a sobriety test then write you a ticket for DWBD?" She stopped dancing. With an ill-tempered look, she placed her hands on her hips while leaning to her right. She mean-mugged Maleek.

"What the hell is a DWBD?" she asked.

"Drinking while being dumb," he answered with a smirk on his face.

"Fuck you, Maleek! Don't worry about your ride home. Troy agreed to follow you to Amy's house. Also, keep your cornball jokes to your own pathetic self. I'm trying to have fun tonight. I know you have some cigars on you. A pothead keeps wraps with them. Just like a crackhead keeps a pipe with them. Here, take this sack and make yourself useful. Go roll up a blunt." She handed him a weed sack that she had bought from Troy. "I know you're good at rolling a blunt up. Hell, you practice every morning, rolling up them breakfast burritos."

Maleek glanced at her. "Haha, very funny," he replied. He then walked away to find Jake, to ask him for some privacy to roll a blunt.

"Is everything going to plan?" asked Amy.

"Yep, Troy knows not to follow Maleek to your house," answered Tawanna.

After scanning the dance floor, he spotted Jake strolling into the kitchen. He was following a White guy. Maleek began to press through the hyped crowd of people dancing. He slowly made his way back across the living room toward the kitchen. He caught up with his old high school buddy and the unknown White guy.

The two of them heard Maleek trekking behind them. They ceased from kissing once he entered the kitchen. "Maleek! What's going on, buddy? You need a drink?" asked Jake.

Maleek paused in his tracks. Then he wondered why Jake and this White guy with long curly hair and an anorexic build were alone in the kitchen, standing very close to one another. They dispersed, putting space between them. Maleek began to ponder about what Romme speculated about Jake being gay. He remembered all the girls in high school that Jake had on his jock. Any notion of him being gay quickly slipped away from his mind. "Yeah, I could use another drink." Jake began to make him a shot. "What I really came to ask you for was…" Jake quickly handed him the shot glass full of alcohol, suspending him from talking as he quickly downed the shot.

Jake felt uneasy. He thought Maleek was going to ask him about being a homosexual. With butterflies in his stomach, the tension was evident in his face. He wasn't ready to tell his old friend about his sex preference.

"Wow! That's some strong alcohol. I felt hair growing on my chest. Oh! What I was going to ask you was, is there a place where I can roll a blunt up?" asked Maleek.

"Hell yeah, there is. May I smoke with you?"

"Of course, bro, this is your house."

"Go upstairs, the first room to your left. Feel free to play some music up there. I have all the old stuff that we used to listen to." The skinny guy that looked like a wannabe woman elbowed Jake in his side. "Oh! Maleek, let me introduce you to Mike. A very good friend of mine."

Mike crossed his arms as he gave Jake an angry look. Jake normally referred to him as Molly. He was embarrassed to admit that in front of Maleek. Unfolding his arms, the feminine-looking man put his sight on Maleek, then extended his arm to shake hands. "Nice to meet you, Maleek."

Damn! This motherfucker sounds like a bitch, thought Maleek while shaking hands with him. *This dude reminds me of them boys in prison*, he said in his mind. In prison, "boys" were a slang name known for homosexuals. After releasing hands, Maleek fixed him another shot. "Give me ten minutes, then come upstairs. I should be done rolling up the weed."

"Okay, I'll be there, bro," said Jake. Maleek turned around to leave the kitchen. He downed the shot and sat the glass on the cabinet. At the entrance of the living room, he paused to look upon the crowd. Amy and Tawanna were dancing together. Amy glanced in his direction; she made eye contact with him. He continued to scan the dance floor. He saw Troy selling weed far off in a corner of the room. Amanda stood by him like a bodyguard. Still looking around the living room, he saw Romme dancing with Nia. Maleek shook his head side to side, then proceeded to walk toward the stairway. Amy left Tawanna on the dance floor to pursue him. He made it to the smoking room upstairs and entered, then swiped the door behind him with a flick of the wrist in a backward motion to close it. He heard a thumping noise.

"Ouch!" yelped Amy, holding her forehead. The swinging door had smacked her head. He spun around fast to see who it was.

"Amy! Are you okay?" In a hurry, he approached her to make sure she was all right. He removed her hands from her forehead. Just a red spot appeared on her for head, no cuts or blemishes. "You sure have a hard head."

"Hm! Thanks, I guess."

"Why were you sneaking up behind me?" wondered Maleek with a smile on his face.

"I wasn't creeping on you. I was trying to catch up with you. To see what you were doing. What are you doing up here?" she asked.

He sat down in a chair stationed in front of a table, then pulled out a weed sack along with a pack of cigars. "I'm rolling up some good green, Mean Gene."

With a baffled look, she glanced at him. "Who's Mean Gene?"

"An old school wrestler."

"Oh yeah, I remember. Randy Savage used to say that all the time. Haha," she giggled. She then staggered over toward him. She was completely wasted. She almost tumbled to the floor; he jumped up and caught her. She looked up at him and kissed him. "My hero," she mumbled.

A big grin appeared on his face as he stared her in the eyes. She was also smiling. He lifted her to her feet, then sat back down. "I suggest you sit down somewhere. I'm going to let your ass fall to the floor next time," he said.

"That's jacked up," she replied. She grabbed a chair and sat close to him.

"Last thing I need is for you to fall and hurt yourself, then somebody walk through that door and accuse me of hitting a White woman. They'll call the police, then haul my Black ass to jail without hearing my side of the story."

Amy stared at him, then leaned on him, showing how drunk she was. "You're so funny, Maleek, but the year is 2022, not twenty-twenty," she mumbled in a boozer tone.

He stopped rolling up the weed, then turned his head. There she was, face-to-face with him. If either one of them moved an inch forward. They would be locking lips. He wanted to scoot her over a little bit, but weed residue was sticking to his fingertips. She started cheesing again. "You mean the year 1920. Hell, your breath smells like MD 20/20. What have you been drinking?" he asked.

With her right arm wrapped around his shoulders, she took her left hand and pressed her index finger up against his nose, pushing on it like a button. "No! I wasn't drinking MD 20/20, Maleek! It was vodka! When you finish wrapping that grass up, may I take a toke?" she asked.

He glanced at her. "I don't think that would be a good idea. You're already babbling like a wino." He completed one blunt and started rolling up the second one.

"You're just mad cuz I'm in the groove. Don't be a masturbator, be a calculator."

Maleek busted out in laughter. "You mean, don't be a hater, be congratulator."

"Yeah! That's what I was saying." She then began looking around the room. Jake had a lot of posters of celebrities on his room wall. She started announcing names of all the celebrities she was observing. "Tom Cruise, Tom Brady, Denzel Washington, Brad Pitt, Morris Chestnut, Mark Wahlberg, LL Cool J."

He started chuckling. "How is it possible that you can't get the year right? Yet you can pronounce all those names."

"Some of them have their shirts off," she replied.

"You wanna take your shirt off. You better not," he commanded.

"No! Look," she shouted as she pointed at the wall. His eyes followed where she was pointing. He saw Arnold Schwarzenegger on the wall as the Terminator in tight leather. David Beckham, Alex Rodriguez. Wesley Snipes as the character Blade. Many more posters were on the wall. Maleek began to believe what Romme was trying to tell him earlier about Jake being gay. He was done rolling up the second blunt. All of a sudden, Jake and Mike entered the room.

"Maleek! I've been searching for you. I told you to use the first room to your left, not your right," said Jake. He felt ashamed; he did not want Maleek to see all these posters of men draped on the room wall.

"My bad, bro, it must be the alcohol. What's wrong with this room?" asked Maleek, pretending as if he didn't think anything of all the famous studs modeling on the wall.

"Hm! Nothing, nothing at all," he answered with a bewildered look on his face.

Mike began to whisper in Jake's ear. "Baby, you need to let him know the truth about you. Don't be ashamed of yourself, or me." His voice sounded like a small woman.

"I will when I'm ready to. Don't rush me," he retorted under his breath. He then shoved Mike, a.k.a. Molly, away from his ear.

"Huh!" Mike muttered while covering his mouth, appalled by the way Jake was behaving in front of his old pal. Teardrops began to mobilize within his eye sockets.

Amy's eyes started to accumulate tears also. "I feel your pain, honey." She then stood up to go and hug him. She wobbled as she attempted to find her balance.

Maleek grabbed her waist. "Girl! You tipsy. Sit your drunk ass down. Is everything okay, Jake?" he asked while simultaneously placing Amy back in her chair.

Amy softly touched the side of Maleek's face, caressing his right cheek. "Hm! I like it when you're aggressive." He was irritated with her drunkenness, but he was also drunk. Yet he knew how to control himself under the influence of alcohol. He couldn't control his laughter, though. He was chuckling at Amy. He had never seen her plastered like this before.

"Y'all ready to smoke?" asked Maleek. All three of them answered yes. He then told Jake to go fetch Tawanna, Romme, Troy, and Amanda. He agreed to round them up and bring them to the room. He exited the room. His girl Molly, a.k.a. Mike, followed him. He shut the door behind him.

"Amy! You're fucked up already. I don't think I should let you hit this weed. If you puke, you better be able to clean yourself."

"That's not fair! I like to puff the magic dragon. You're my delighted diver. You suppose to take care of me," she replied. *Man, she's wasted*, he thought.

"I'm supposed to make sure you get home safely, not clean the shit in between your ass crack."

Jake and Mike came back into the room. Tawanna, Romme, and Nia strolled in behind them. Nia shut the door behind her. Maleek gave Nia a funny stare. "What is Medusa doing here? We're trying to get stoned, not get turned into stone."

"Shut up, bitch, or I'll come over there and slap the piss shit out of your ass again," shouted Nia.

"I invited her to smoke with us," informed Romme.

Maleek tucked his upper lip and hung his bottom lip out more. He gazed at Romme with a facial expression of disapproval. "Where's Amanda and Troy?"

"Troy said he has money to make," explained Jake.

"Oh well, more for us. Catch, Tawanna," shouted Maleek. He tossed one of the cigars to her. He also grabbed her weed bag and wrapped it shut. He then threw the sack at her like a baseball. It hit her on the head, then fell to the floor. Before she picked it up, she mean-mugged her brother while waving a closed fist, indicating she wanted to punch him. He had a smirk on his face. "Spark your blunt when I spark mine. May the euphoric feelings begin." He placed the blunt in his mouth, then reached in his pocket for a lighter.

"I got it, Maleek," said Amy. She already had a lighter in her hand.

With the cigar hanging out of his mouth, Maleek began to chat in a gibberish tone. "Oh! About time you do something right." With the lighter in her hand, she slowly extended her arm toward the blunt hanging from his lips. Despite sitting next to him, she had difficulty reaching her target. Tawanna had already ignited her blunt. Finally, Amy started clicking on the lighter to produce a flame. Maleek began puffing on the blunt to even out the cherry. Thick smoke began to float around the room. "Okay, you can take the lighter away," gibbered Maleek.

With a grin on her face, Amy stared at the flame while it connected to the front tip of the cigar. She was amused by the tiny fire she controlled. With the blunt dangling from his mouth, he noticed Amy burning it. He began to shout rapidly and incoherently. "Amy! Put that damn lighter up."

"Oh! I'm sorry," she responded. She nonchalantly lowered the lighter. In a sluggish manner, she inched the igniter back toward herself. Her eyeballs were still captivated by the lighter, not releasing the button. The flame was still on when she lowered it down, by Maleek's chin.

"Man! Is it just me or is it hot in here?" asked Maleek.

"Maleek! The bottom of your beard is on fire," yelled Romme as he pointed at him. His pupils sank in a hurry to the bottom of his eye sockets. Maleek quickly passed the blunt to Jake. He then yelped as he started patting on his goatee to put out the small fire.

"I'll save you, Maleek," shouted Amy. She stood up and was very unbalanced in her stance as she wobbled.

Tawanna busted out laughing at her brother. "That's what yo ass gets for hitting me on my head with my own weed sack." Nia joined in on the laughter. Amy trotted to a dresser; she clutched a cup in her hand. It already had some type of liquid in it. She spun around, then began trotting toward Maleek.

"No, Amy! Don't use that cup!" shouted Jake. "It's not water."

"Ouch!" Amy lost her balance, falling forward, landing directly in Maleek's lap. She stood up on her knees. It seemed as if she was giving a blow job to him. Her forward momentum caused the substance within the cup to eject out of it, flying, splashing onto his face.

"Ah!" screamed Maleek like a little schoolgirl. The liquid that spattered on him was alcohol, causing the fire to intensify.

"Run to the bathroom! It's to your left," shouted Jake. With a fireball attached to the bottom of his goatee, Maleek roughly shoved Amy out of his lap as if she had bitten him on the penis. He sprinted to the restroom while hollering like a cow in a slaughter going wrong.

"Ha!" complained Amy as she lay on the floor looking up. "Did anyone get the license plate number to that truck?" she asked while pointing at the ceiling.

Tawanna handed Romme the blunt, then rose out of her chair to help her best friend and aided her to her seat. "Don't worry, girl, you're okay. I also got the license's plate number from that vehicle. It wasn't a truck. It was a Pinto."

"What is it? I'm going to report a hit 'n' run on that asshole." Everybody was laughing because of her drunkenness.

"It's Jailbird 42969-177."

Amy looked confused. "Say what? It was Big Bird? No way! Big Bird wouldn't do that." Tawanna sat back down in her seat, rejoining the blunt rotation. With an angry facial expression, Maleek walked back into the room. He parked in his seat, right next to Amy. He turned his head and stared at Amy. He looked like he had gotten into a fight with Freddie Krueger during a house fire.

While the blunt was being passed around, everybody in the room was pointing and laughing at him. Mike extended his hand to give Amy the blunt. Maleek intercepted it from her. "Ha! It's my turn to hit the chronic," she whined.

Maleek took a puff from it, then blew smoke in her face. While closing her eyes, she drew her head back as if she was dodging a punch. "No! You're already fucked up. You're not touching this weed," he said.

"Let her hit it, Maleek," yelled Tawanna. "You're not her daddy!"

"Look what she did to my beard, goddamn it. I should press charges on her ass."

"If she wants to smoke, then let her." He didn't agree with Tawanna, but he still gave Amy the blunt. She smiled from ear to ear like a kid off punishment. She reached her free hand toward Maleek.

He was unaware of her advancement. Once making contact with his chin, he flinched; he was jumpy from all the other incidents that occurred.

"You're so sweet, Maleek," she said, petting his chin like a dog. For a minute, she kept rubbing his chin while holding the blunt. "Your beard is patchy. Is everything okay?"

"If you're not going to smoke, pass the green. And please stop rubbing my chin." She listened to him. She sat straight up in her chair, then braced herself. Maleek gave her a funny look. "It's a blunt, not a collage exam. Hit the damn thing, would you." With an upside-down smile and contracted eyebrows displaying displeasure, she jiggled her head from side to side, twitching her neck from left to right. It looked like her head was bouncing from shoulder to shoulder.

She began to sing while doing so. "I'm a little teapot, short and stout!" Everyone in the room was giggling.

In frustration, Maleek rested his palm on his forehead as he leaned down overlooking his lap. "You're going to get a crick in your neck if you keep doing that," he mentioned. She finally placed the cigar in her mouth. She was still jerking her head side to side while staring at him. She inhaled deeply on the weed. Her coughing erupted like a volcano. It seemed as if she was choking. She stretched her arm out to hand Maleek the blunt while coughing.

He took it from her. While toking on it, he stood up and started patting her on the back to help her catch her breath. Romme was watching Maleek and Amy from across the room. He continued to laugh, until he noticed some of the posters in the background where Maleek was standing.

With his mouth wide open, he started to look around the room in a circular motion. Silently, he began naming out names in his mind. Antonio Banderas, Patrick Swayze, and Sylvester Stallone as the character in *Tango & Cash*. Bo Jackson, Chuck Norris, and Herschel Walker. *What the hell?* he pondered.

It was obvious to Jake that Romme had found out about his sexual preference. He stood up from his seat to make an announcement. He cleared his throat. By this time, everyone in the room was watching him. He passed the blunt to Tawanna. "Excuse me, everybody, I have a secret to tell. Before I do, I would like to apologize for keeping it hidden." With all eyes on him, he scanned the room.

Mike rubbed him on the back. "Go ahead, it's going to be okay."

Jake cleared his throat one more time, then stirred up the courage he needed. "I'm gay."

Chapter 21

Round 1

"I told you he was a faggot," said Romme.

"Don't say that word, you motherfucker," shouted Mike in a proper tone. His name was Mike, but he sounded like a woman named Molly.

Romme stood up from his seat. "Shut yo little delicate, gentle, ladylike, hems-injecting ass up. I'll whoop yo maidenly, tender, fair-seeming ass." Mike stared at him with his mouth wide open. "Yeah! That's right, punk, stay in your place, boy! Just like a little be-yatch!"

"Oh, hell naw," fussed Mike. "Jake! You better control your friend before I kick his ass." His voice sounded like Taylor Swift.

"Please, Romme, calm down. Molly! Relax, baby. He doesn't mean it like that, we're old friends," explained Jake.

Usually, Maleek was the smart-ass with a remark to say. He had seen this type of behavior in prison. He really liked Jake a lot, so he kept his opinions to himself. He peeped at the clock. "How! It's 3:15 a.m. We better get a move on." He tried using a departure as a way to break up this dispute. He helped Amy to her feet and put the half-smoked blunt in the ashtray. "Let's go home, everybody. It's time to leave," he demanded.

With the other blunt in her mouth, Tawanna stood up and started dialing a number on her cell phone. She was calling her ride,

Jamal. Maleek began escorting Amy out of the room. Romme, Nia, and Tawanna followed him.

Before they could exit the room, Romme paused and gazed at Jake. Covered in shame, Jake looked down at the floor. "What happened to you, man? You were a stud in high school."

"He's still a stud," said Molly.

"This monster you call Molly ain't no woman. He has a link in between his legs. Just like me and you."

"Get the hell out of here and leave my man alone," shouted Molly.

"I can't help it, it's what I desire," replied Jake.

"Did this atrocity slip a molly in your drink the first time y'all met? If so, it's okay. You don't have to stay with it. Please tell me you're not letting this swamp thing stick its johnson in your booty hole," pleaded Romme as he tried to cajole his old friend from being gay.

"That's it! I'm going to rub your ass with my foot until it shines," declared Molly as he started popping his knuckles.

"Oh, you wanna dance, huh. Come on, I'm going to show you that this is a man's world," Romme responded. He started prancing around the room in a circle while throwing jabs like Muhammad Ali. Everybody leaving turned around to watch.

"Yeah! We're going to find out who's the bitch now," shouted Molly in a deep, thunderous voice. He sounded like Taylor Swift earlier in the night; now his voice sounded like a seven-foot-tall man. It suddenly changed and sounded like the actor's voice on the All-State commercials. Romme stopped prancing around like a deer, coming to a standstill. Fear overtook him; it was apparent in his facial expression. *O Lord, what have I got myself into*, he thought to himself. He glanced at Maleek as if he was going to help. Maleek shrugged his shoulders.

With his left hand held up close to his chin, his right hand swaying next to his right hip, Molly was slowly nearing toward him in a southpaw stance. Romme reacted by holding up his dukes like a traditional boxer. They began to circle one another as they sized each other up. *Bam!* Molly threw a quick left jab, striking his opponent on the nose.

Romme stepped back, then brushed his hand against the bottom of his nostrils. He saw a speck of blood on his palm. "It's on now, you sissy. You wanna fight? Let's rumble," he shouted in a wild rage.

He busted off in a rush with his arms wide open, trying to grab on to Molly. "Huh!" he yelped.

Molly had kicked him in the stomach once he made it within reach.

While Romme was bending over holding his tummy, trying to regain his breath, Molly walked behind him. Troy and Amanda entered the room. Troy quickly pulled out his cell phone to record the quarrel. "He's going to hump him in the ass," yelled Amy. They all glanced at her, including Molly.

"Is this all you can muster up, motherfucker?" shouted Molly in a prissy tone of voice. He then kicked him in the ass like a game of kickball.

"Oh snap! That queer just literally kicked Romme's ass," blurted Troy.

Romme flopped forward on his belly. Molly pounced on his back, similar to a jockey jumping on a horse. He poured down a flurry of punches to the back of his skull. Romme covered up the back of his head with his arms, better than a turtle ducking in its shell. Molly began to take his time with striking, carefully picking his blows with accuracy, to no avail. He couldn't make contact with his opponent's noggin because he was blocking too well.

"You can't hide from me, you punk motherfucker," cursed Molly in a squeamish tone of voice. He then wrapped his arm around his contender's neck, placing him in a rear naked choke.

"We got to break this shit up. He's getting manhandled. Jake! Get that fucking goblin off him," cursed Maleek.

Jake followed his command. He scurried over to the belligerent brawlers, then tapped Molly on the shoulder. "That's enough, baby, let him go," demanded Jake. Romme was snoring by this time, sound asleep. Molly released the tight constriction squeezing his neck, then stood over his snoozing victim. He reached down and slapped him on the back of the head, then spat on him. Jake grabbed him and dragged him away. Maleek picked up an empty cup then went into the restroom. He filled it up with cold water. He walked over to a slumbering Romme and arched over to look him in the face.

He tossed the water on him, splashing him in the face. "Huh! Not my gumdrop buttons," blurted Romme as he lifted his head.

"What the fuck were you dreaming about, man? Get yo ass up so we can leave," said Maleek.

Romme jumped up to his feet fast. He spotted Molly. "You lucky I'm drunk because otherwise I would've served yo ass on a platter." Instantly, Molly became aggressive as he tried to get to Romme. Jake was holding him back. Romme trotted out the room, scared.

While Jake restrained Molly in the room, everyone else began walking downstairs. Amanda and Troy were giggling so loud and long, it seemed like they were weeping. Nia was nursing Romme's ego. "It's okay, you were drunk. You'll see that punk again."

Troy pointed at him while laughing hard. "Ah-ha, you let that boy beat you up like that."

"Man! Y'all keep this on the down low. Don't tell nobody what happened. I was intoxicated," explained Romme as an excuse to why a homosexual had kicked his ass.

Romme led the seven of them through the thick crowd of people on the living room dance floor. The party was still hyped at 3:40 a.m. "Don't worry, Romme. We won't say a word to anyone," said Troy while Amanda and he were viewing the recorded fight on his cell phone over and over. The two of them trailed last.

All seven of them stepped outside the house party. A squad car was parked on the street in front of the house. Maleek was first to notice the cop. He paused. "Damn! We have weed on us. Maybe we should go back in the house to wait this cop out. Just in case he fucks with us." Tawanna kept walking straight toward the patrol car. "Where you going?" asked her brother.

"Relax, booty hole licker. It's my ride, Jamal," answered Tawanna. Jamal hopped out of the driver side and sat in the passenger seat. Tawanna jumped in the driver seat. "Maleek, Maleek, what you gone do? What you gone do when we come for you?" she sung out loud over the PA sound transmitter on top of the cop car. She then drove off with the flashing siren lights on.

Romme walked Nia to her car. Troy and Amanda loaded up in his Tahoe, waiting for Romme. Maleek gently placed Amy in the passenger side of her car. "Don't leave me here," cried Amy as she clutched on to Maleek's shirt.

"Calm down, silly Billy. I'm not going nowhere," replied Maleek as he yanked her hand away from his shirt. He shut the car door. She put her arms up and placed her palms on the window, then smudged her lips on the glass and blew her breath, fogging the window. Her cheeks looked like a blow fish every time she inhaled then exhaled. She looked like a big kid doing so.

Chapter 22

Just Us Two

Maleek laughed as he walked toward Troy's vehicle. After chatting with Nia, Romme hopped in the back seat.

"Don't forget to follow me to Amy's house," said Maleek.

"I'm right behind you, cuz," Troy replied. Maleek turned around to get in the vehicle with Amy.

"Maleek! Why didn't you help me in there?" asked Romme.

"It was a one-on-one fight," answered Maleek.

"That's fucked up, man!"

"Naw! What's fucked up is you got whooped by that boy. You figured you'd win the fight just because he likes to put a flute in his mouth. And I'm not talking about the instrument. I bet you want make fun of me getting spanked by my momma anymore."

"We were kids then, I couldn't help it."

"If you were in prison, I couldn't have done anything for you. Plus, you would've been raped. That boy kicked your ass, but I wasn't going to let him fondle your balls or toss your salad while you were asleep," explained Maleek. With a smile on his face, he turned around and jumped in the driver seat of Amy's car. She reached out and touched his cheek and held it.

"I knew you would come back for me," chanted Amy.

He glanced at her while shaking his head side to side. "How many drinks have you had tonight?"

She released the side of his face. With a confused look on her face, she said, "I'm not sure." He revved up the engine; after a minute, he drove off. Troy followed behind him with his music playing loudly. His radio was extremely loud. Maleek felt like he was sitting in the Tahoe.

While crossing over Highway 161 on the Northgate bridge, the music suddenly faded away. He stared in his rearview mirror. Troy exited Northgate onto Highway 161, headed toward the 360 freeway on the way to Arlington. *What the hell is he doing?* asked Maleek in his mind. Ten minutes later, he parked in the driveway of Amy's crib. He opened the door to get out of the car.

"Maleek! Don't leave me again," shouted Amy as she tried to grab him. Her seat belt held her back. He shut the car door, then looked through the window. She had her face resting within the palms of her hands, crying.

"No more alcohol for this girl," said Maleek. He walked over to the passenger-side door and opened it. She lifted her head to look at him.

"My dark knight. I knew you wouldn't abandon me." While looking at her with a crazy look, he unbuckled her seat belt. He helped her get out of the vehicle and escorted her into her parents' house. He led her to her room and laid her down in the bed. She fell asleep fast. Maleek exited the house with her keys to lock the door behind him. He dialed Troy's cell phone number; Troy didn't answer it. *I'm going to kick his ass,* he thought. It was 4:05 a.m.

He went next door to his parents' house. He called his dad's cell phone, but Tyrone didn't answer. He had to knock on the door because he didn't have a key. He had to wake both of his parents up. He rang the doorbell. A few minutes went by; no one opened the door.

Chapter 23

Oh Shit

He turned around to walk and think about what he was going to do next. Unexpectedly, the front door swung open. He spun around to go inside. "Huh!" mumbled Maleek in shock as he jumped. There stood his father butt naked with an erection, wearing a dodo bird mask. Maleek stood there not saying a word.

"Boy! You just gone stand there and look stupid, or do you want to come inside? What the hell are you doing here this late anyways?" asked Tyrone.

"You scared the shit out of me with that mask on. You know you're nude, right?"

"Me and yo momma was knockin' boots until yo cock-blocking ass showed up knocking on my door. Boy! Bring yo Black ass in here. Got me standing in the open butt ass naked talking to you."

"Hm! Don't worry, Pops, I'll find somewhere else to go. You might accidently stab me with your knife down there pointing at me."

"Knife! You mean my samurai sword," bragged Tyrone.

"I'm surprised that you still have enough testosterone. At your age you'd normally be asleep around this time."

"Just because I'm wearing a dodo bird mask doesn't mean my sex life is extinct too. Boy, if you not coming inside, I'm shutting this door. It's getting cold. I feel a draft hitting my balls."

"Go ahead, naked jabber, I have somewhere to go," insisted Maleek. Tyrone slammed the front door, then locked it. He decided to go back to Amy's house. He locked the door behind him. He lay down on the couch and went to sleep. The time now was 7:14 a.m. on a Friday.

Maleek abruptly awoke from his sleep. He heard keys jiggling by the front door. "Oh shit! Todd and Alice are home," he muttered. Todd and Alice were Amy's parents; they were out of town for Thanksgiving. They were back home now. He swiftly rose off the sofa, then bolted into Amy's room. He closed the room door behind him and then hid on the other side of Amy's bed. She was still asleep.

Her parents opened the room door. "She's sleep," whispered Alice.

"We should get some snooze ourselves, honey," replied Todd.

"Yeah, you're right, sweetie. We'll speak to her once she wakes up." They left, closing the door behind them. Maleek swiped the sweat off his forehead while taking a deep breath.

He was clueless on what to do; plus he was exhausted. He snatched a pillow from the bed and lay down on the floor. Two hours later, the time now was 9:17 a.m. Amy woke up with a monstrous hangover. She looked around, wondering how she made it home. She grabbed her cell phone out of her pocket, then dialed her best friend's number.

"Hello," answered Tawanna as she picked up the phone.

"Ha, girl. I'm sitting here thinking to myself in my room. How in the blueberry muffin did I make it home? I can't recall nothing from last night," explained Amy.

"You don't remember our plan. We told Troy not to follow you and Maleek so you could get him to your house. My brother should be there with you."

"Oh yeah! I remember now. But my clothes are still on, and Maleek is nowhere to be found."

"If he's not there with you, I don't know where he's at. Unless he went to our parents' house."

"If he is next door, he's still holding my keys. I can't believe he didn't take advantage of me. I was hoping I'd wake up nude," she explained.

"Any other normal guy would have. He's my brother, but this needs to be known. I think Maleek is gay. He probably likes hairy bootyholes better. It must be tighter than some pussy," explained Tawanna.

"No way! You think so? Women have booty holes too."

"Yeah! That's true, but he probably wants to manhandle another guy. Then he probably likes to get his ass rammed into."

"Ma'am! Place your hands against the wall and spread your legs," demanded Jamal. Amy realized she was on speakerphone.

"Yes, Officer. Are you going to pat search me?" asked Tawanna.

"You have me on speakerphone?" said Amy.

"Tawanna is right, Amy. Maleek is probably gay," agreed Jamal. He started patting down Tawanna. "What's this, ma'am?" he questioned as he pulled out a weed sack from her pocket.

"Please, Officer, don't take me to prison. I'll do anything you want me to," begged Tawanna.

"Did you just try to bribe me, ma'am? That's it, place your hands on the bed rail," he commanded.

"Hm! Would you like me to call you later, girl?" asked Amy. She heard the sound of chains through her cell phone. *Click, click*, he handcuffed both of Tawanna's wrists, then cuffed her to the bed railing with two pairs of handcuffs. He unbuckled her pants, slowly pulling them down to her ankles. "Does this mean you're going to accept my bribe, Officer?" asked Tawanna.

"Hush your mouth, you scum bucket, before I charge you with obstruction of justice and haul your nice round booty to prison," shouted Jamal. He began rubbing her ass.

"Oh! Yes, Officer."

"You have two options, ma'am. I can take you to prison, or you can let me wax that ass from behind. Don't try to trick me either. I'm a cop, no one will believe you."

"Please, Officer! I can't go to prison. I'll do whatever you want me to do."

"Good answer, dirtbag. Now shut your filthy mouth. I'm going to roll a blunt on your ass first."

"Hm! I'm going to hang up the phone. I don't want to have to go into witness protection," said Amy. She ended the phone call and tossed her cell phone on the bed. She rose up to get out of bed. While dangling her legs from the edge of the mattress, she stared out the window. Then she hopped off the bed.

"Ah!" yelped Maleek in pain. She had landed right on his private part, waking him up.

"Oh my god. I'm sorry, Maleek. I didn't know you were down there," she said while stepping off his balls. He rolled over to his side while holding his crotch.

"Damn, Amy, you set me on fire last night. Now you stomp on my balls. What have I done to you?"

"I'm sorry. Why were you sleeping on the floor?"

"I was sleeping on the sofa until I heard your parents coming through the front door."

Chapter 24

Hip-Hop

Amy looked surprised. "My parents! They weren't supposed to be home until Sunday," she said while extending her hand to Maleek to help him up. He grabbed her hand and began to stand up.

Suddenly, her parents knocked on the room door.

"Huh!" mumbled Maleek. She threw him back down to the floor.

"Come in," shouted Amy.

The door swung open; her parents stood in the doorway. She approached them and hugged both of them. "I thought I heard you speaking with somebody," said Todd.

"I was chatting with Tawanna on the phone," replied Amy.

"How is she doing? We haven't seen her since high school. Speaking of the Johnson family. Did you hear about her brother Maleek? He served time in a federal penitentiary for bank robbery while you were in college. His mom and dad are very wealthy. I can't understand why he couldn't just ask them for money. He was such a sweet little kid. I never thought he'd do something like that," explained Alice.

"Maleek was a good kid. It must be that hip-hop music. It makes these young Black men go hot under the collar. So youthful. So ferocious! Curse that rap music," said Todd.

Amy gazed at him. "Dad! You listen to rap music yourself. Ice Cube is your favorite rapper."

"Hm! Hm! Well, you know I listen to rap music for a reason. I have Black clients and, hm! Ice Cube is more considered an MC rather than a rapper. As a psychologist, I listen to Ice Cube because his music helps me understand the Black man's perspective of America. Ever since the Black Lives Matter movement, I've been counseling more African Americans. This country has not treated Blacks fairly at all from day one when they arrived in America. Their rage against the law is very understandable," explained her dad.

"You know, Pops, that's a good excuse for your love of gangster rap. You do know there's a difference between rap and gangster rap."

"Well, yes, of course. I need to hear the true art form of hip-hop. Its catchy lyrics give me a vivid picture of what's really going on in the Black communities of North America."

"What about your 2 Live Crew CD? Does Luke help you with your African American studies? Better yet. What about your Sir Mix-a-Lot album?"

"Well, I do like big butts, and your mother has a fat ass." He then slapped Alice on her bottom.

Alice's face blushed red. "Todd! Act your age."

"Okay, I'm guilty. I love hip-hop music. Your mom and I like to jam Luke when we—ouch!" He mumbled.

Alice had jabbed him in the gut. "That's enough, Todd!" she shouted.

Amy had a grin on her face.

"You know, sweetie, you should talk to Maleek. Grasp his evaluation of how it feels to be Black in America. As a rookie psychologist, that might help you. You've been knowing him your entire life. It'll be easier to interview someone you know," explained her dad.

"We're so proud of you, honey, for following in our footsteps. We can talk about that later, though. We're headed to the grocery store. Would you like for us to get you something?" asked her mother.

"Mom, you know I'm moving into my apartment tomorrow. I'll purchase my own food."

"You just came back home from college. Stay here with us for a while. We missed you, honey."

"I missed y'all too, Mom, but I need my own space. Plus, I start my new job on Monday. I'm moving to Arlington, where it's located. Don't worry, it's only twenty-five minutes away. I'll visit all the time."

"If you insist. We're going to catch a movie before we go shopping. If you change your mind about us getting you anything, give us a call."

"What movie are you two going to see?"

"*Morbius*. Of course, your father picked it. He's been mad buggin' me to go watch it."

"We have fourteen minutes before our movie starts. We better go," suggested her father.

Chapter 25

Wet

"Before you move out, think about it, Amy. You could save some money staying here with us," advised Alice.

"I will, Mom. Go enjoy your movie." They both spun around and exited the front door, locking it behind them. Maleek stood up to his feet, then tossed Amy's keys on her bed. "Sorry about that, Maleek."

"Are you apologizing for last night? Or for throwing me down to the floor? After five hundred years of slavery, White people are still abusing Black people."

"No, you didn't, that's not fair. I was the only one not laughing at you when your mother was spanking you with a stick while you were nude. You recall that?"

He began to shake; he regained his composure. "Please don't remind me. I've been permanently scarred by that horrific event. I can't believe your dad told you to study me like an animal or something."

"You know he didn't mean it like that. My dad has always liked you."

"Yeah! Your dad has always been good in my book. At least he knows where us young Black men are coming from. What time is it?" he asked.

Amy looked at her cell phone screen. "Nine fifty a.m."

"Do you mind giving me a ride home? I don't know why that dingbat Troy stopped following us last night."

"Do you mind if I take a shower first?" she asked.

"No, not at all. I'll be waiting in the living room." He exited the room, closing the door behind him. He sat down on the sofa. Not wanting to watch television, he relaxed on the couch in silence. He noticed a cell phone lying on the living room table set but paid it no mind. It began ringing; he arched over to glance at it. The caller ID read Alice.

Todd had forgotten his cell phone. Maleek sat back on the sofa, ignoring the phone. As he started to doze off, fifteen minutes passed by. He heard keys jiggling by the front door. He took off like a rocket from the couch into Amy's room in a hurry, then shut the door behind him.

Todd came into the house to retrieve his cell phone. He grabbed it, then left out the front door.

"I'm so sorry, Amy. I had no choice but to barge into your room. Your dad came back for his cell phone," said Maleek. There she stood in the buff, about to put on her panties. She turned around and faced him. With his mouth wide open, he quickly got an erection while gazing at her well-formed body. He spun around to walk out the room.

"Wait! Don't go out. Let me check to see if my dad left," said Amy. She marched straight toward his direction completely nude. He couldn't take his eyes off her. She gripped his wrist and moved him from the front of the door. She then poked her head out the door to survey the living room. Todd was gone.

She closed the door and then pinned Maleek's back up against it. "I don't see anybody out there," said Amy.

"I promise you that someone came through that front door. I knew you were in the shower. I wouldn't infringe on you like that," he refuted. Without any warning, she kissed him on the lips. In the moment of heated passion, they stared one another in the eyes, then began kissing wildly. She started stripping off his clothes while doing so. He paused in the middle of their advancing sexual excitement.

"What's wrong?" she wondered while tossing his shirt to the floor.

"I haven't brushed my teeth or taken a shower since yesterday," he replied.

"Catch me," she said as she jumped up on him. He caught her in midair; she wrapped her legs around his waist. His palms were gripped tight on her ass cheeks for leverage. "Carry me to the bathroom," she demanded while kissing on his neck and shoulders. He began toting her to the bathroom. During the front piggyback ride, she was sucking on his neck hard, leaving a hickey on him.

She unwrapped her legs from around his hips, setting her feet on the floor. Then she picked up a bottle of mouthwash. She handed it to him and smiled, indicating to him that his breath does stink.

With a grin on his face, he snatched it from her. While untwisting the top, she aggressively unbuckled his jeans, letting them drop to his ankles. His boxers came off next.

While gargling the mouthwash in his mouth, Amy clutched onto his rod like a joystick. "Ha!" He flinched with mouth rinse in his mouth. He gargled loudly as the pace of rinsing his mouth picked up from excitement. She held on to the tip of his pecker and led him to the shower. With her free hand, she adjusted the temperature of the water, then dragged him in the shower with her.

He spat the mouth rinse out as the water began to produce steam on the shower door. Their attachment seemed like it was meant to be as they were loving one another. After twenty minutes of tender love, they cleaned one another.

After exiting the shower and getting dressed, the time was ten thirty-seven on a Friday morning. "You ready to go?" asked Amy.

"Yeah," answered Maleek. The two of them walked out of her parents' house. She locked the front door behind her. They hopped in her car, then began the trip to Arlington. He started contemplating in his head on what had just happened between them. *Damn, I just sold out. I can't let anybody know about us.*

Chapter 26

Watch Out

Fifteen minutes went by as they headed to Arlington. No one spoke a word. "What's the exit, Maleek?" she asked.

"Regal Row," he answered.

"Are you okay?"

"Yeah, of course." Seven minutes later, they arrived at his apartments. She parked a few spaces away from his apartment.

For a moment, they just stared at each other. "Are you going to invite me to see your place?" she asked.

His mouth was wide open as his bottom lip hung out further than the top one. He gazed at her. "Yeah! Why not." *Fuck, I hope Romme is asleep*, he thought in his head. He began peeping out the windows of the vehicle to make sure nobody he knew spotted him. He was embarrassed to be with Amy. If he was seen with a White woman, all the rhetoric of being pro-Black that came off his tongue would make him look like a hypocrite.

"Is everything okay?" she asked.

He was pondering a fast excuse. "Okay, here's the plan."

Amy looked at him like he was crazy. "Plan for what?"

"These apartments are very dangerous. We're going to walk very fast to my apartment. Follow my every move, do exactly as I do. Do you understand?"

She had a frightened look on her face. "Hm! Okay, what kind of dangers are lurking here?"

He nudged one index finger against her lips. "Shh. No questions right now. The longer we sit in this car the more we put ourselves in harm's way." Her eye pupils were staring down and inward at his finger, causing her to look retarded. "You ready?" he asked with his finger still pressed up against her lips. With her pupils still glued on his finger, she nodded her head up and down.

He removed his finger from her lips, then looked around the parking lot again. "On three, we're going to make a break for it. Stay on my heels." She knew that he didn't want anybody to see her with him. Yet she played along with him as if she didn't know what he was doing. She nodded her head okay. He counted to three.

They both hopped out of the car quickly. Amy pushed the car alarm button on her key chain. He took off in a fast stride toward his apartment door. She trailed close behind him in a similar pace. He was peeping behind himself, not paying attention to the front of his path. He stepped off the parking lot onto the sidewalk.

"Watch out," warned Amy.

He quickly faced forward. "Ha!" He was startled as he ran smack-dab into an old lady with a cane, knocking her down to the ground and falling on top of her. He caught himself from landing on top of her with all his weight by catching himself in push-up form. Both of his palms were flat on the ground to the left and right side of her head. While lying on top of her, they made extremely close eye contact. Maleek opened his mouth to apologize and ask the old lady if she was okay.

Before he could, she spoke first. "My name is Betty. You don't have to rape me, sonny. I'll let you wax my ass freely. I haven't had any pleasure in twenty years, but we can't do it outside. My apartment is right there in front of us." She smiled.

Amy covered her mouth with her hand and chuckled.

Maleek stood up to his feet. "Let's keep moving."

"Aren't you going to help Betty back up to her feet?" asked Amy.

"Hell no, leave her freaky ass down there. Besides, if I help her up, she might pickpocket me."

"Your broke ass doesn't have any money to pickpocket. You stupid burger flipper," shouted Betty.

"You hear that anger? Don't let her old age fool you. She's dangerous," explained Maleek. While lying on the ground, unable to stand up by herself, Betty stared Amy in the face and kept blinking.

Amy crossed her arms and leaned to her left. "I'm not moving until you help her back to her feet."

"All right," responded Maleek. He picked up Betty and stood her up, then handed her the cane.

"You're such a strong young man," complimented Betty.

"Yeah, whatever, Golden Girl," replied Maleek as he began walking fast again. Amy pursued him. They made it to his apartment. He unlocked the door; they both entered the apartment. He shut the door behind him. "Welcome to my humble home."

"There's two rooms. You have a roommate."

"Romme is my roommate. His door is closed. He must be asleep. Please have a seat. I'm going to brush my teeth and change clothes. I'll be right back." Amy watched TV while he went to change clothes and clean his teeth. *This place could use a woman's touch*, thought Amy as she looked around the two-bedroom apartment. Maleek came out of his room with a fresh set of clothes on. He sat on the couch a few feet from Amy. "We need to talk about what happened at your house."

Chapter 27

That's Great!

"I'm listening," she replied.

Maleek glanced at her while she was flipping through TV channels. "Well, I was wondering, where do we go from here?"

Amy turned the volume down on the TV as their conversation became serious. She locked eyes with him. "We've known one another since adolescence. You've always been my closest guy friend because of your sister. My parents know and love you. Your mother and father also feel the same way about me. We're meant to be together, Maleek. As a psychologist, I can understand how you feel about race. Prison has given you a divided aspect on race. I might be White, but I love you."

"I'll be honest with you. I've had a crush on you since we were young. When growing up, I saw the world for what it really is. A lot of resentment entered my heart while in prison. I learned the darker side of history of America's treatment toward Africans. Blacks are so messed up in the head from slavery three hundred years ago. We still carry a lot of traits from bondage that mentally affects us."

"I'm sorry about what happened to your people in the past due to my race. I hope we two can start a better future," she explained while touching his cheekbone. They locked eyes and began kissing.

They stopped kissing, then stared one another in the eyes. "I know you're embarrassed to be seen with me. I'll be patient with you and give you time to come around, but I'll also track you down and let it be known about us. You can sprint, but you can't hide," informed Amy as she scooted closer to Maleek to lay on top of his chest.

"I knew you really didn't believe that these apartments are dangerous."

"Yeah! An old lady with a cane named Betty. I'm so scared. Why'd she call you a stupid burger flipper?"

"I work at Mr. Yumburger. She eats there all the time."

"Oh! That makes sense. You asked me where we go from here. We'll start off with boyfriend and girlfriend. Is that okay with you?"

Maleek wrapped his arms around her as they cuddled up together. He kissed her on the side of her cheekbone. "Yeah, that's cool with me."

While the back of her head rested on his chest, she held his right wrist up against herself as they got comfortable. "To help you not feel ashamed of me, we're going to sit right here and cuddle until Romme comes out of that room. That'll be a good start."

Ten seconds later, Romme walked out of the room with Nia trailing him. Romme paused in his tracks as he spotted Maleek and Amy cuddling. A grin appeared on his face. "Ha, Amy, what's up?" said Nia and Romme simultaneously.

"Ha," replied Amy with a smile on her face.

"What's up, Maleek?" greeted Romme.

"I'll tell you what's up. Why did Troy leave me stranded last night? And why did you bring this pterodactyl in our crib?" asked Maleek.

"Who you calling a pterodactyl, you grease junkie," shouted Nia.

"Baby, please stop," begged Romme.

"He started it first."

"Baby! Ain't no infant in here. What in the sausage McMuffin is going on here?" wondered Maleek.

"We need to discuss something," replied Romme.

"It's self-evident that Nia and you are hooking up. There's no need to explain anything to me. When you two were having sex last night, I hope you saw her naked with the lights on. She could have a rod in between those legs. She probably tricked you to enter her asshole undiscovered, using the dark," warned Maleek.

Nia was about to open her mouth to curse him out. "Wait! Please relax, baby, he's just kidding," explained Romme.

"I'll chill because you want me to and that's your friend, but you better put a nozzle on that poodle's mouth," replied Nia.

Romme took a deep breath, then exhaled. "Okay, let's all sit down on the sofa and roll up a blunt. That way I can take my time to discuss with you." He along with Nia sat on the couch, joining Maleek and Amy. She rose off Maleek to sit up straight. Nia sat beside her as Romme and Maleek sat on the outside of them.

Maleek pulled out his weed sack along with a box of cigars. They never discussed anything together that required them to take their time and sit down. For the first time, he was concerned about what could possibly come out of his friend's mouth. He was dumbfounded at the information he was about to receive. Yet he knew it was serious.

While breaking down the weed, Romme glanced at him. "You know how we agreed to renew our lease for the apartment on Tuesday?" he asked.

"Yes, what about it?" answered Maleek. He stopped breaking down the weed to look his friend in the face. Romme was hesitant to open his mouth to respond.

"Go ahead, sweetie, explain yourself," encouraged Nia while rubbing his back.

Romme braced himself to speak up. "I decided not to stay here anymore. I won't be renewing the lease with you. I'm going to move in with Nia at her place."

Maleek leaned over and rested his elbows on his kneecaps while placing his forehead in his palms, looking downward. "I'm sorry, bro! Please don't be upset with me," pleaded Romme. The time now was 11:30 a.m. on a Friday.

Maleek sat up straight. "Don't worry, bro. I'm not mad with you. We're all adults. I don't blame you for wanting to live with a woman, it's normal. Trust me, it sucks living in a small place with a grown-ass man. Especially when you're trapped in the room while your cellmate is taking a shit. I can barely afford to pay my side of the rent. I can't afford to pay for a one-bedroom by myself because of utilities. That's the only thing I'm worried about. I don't want to be forced to move back to my parents' house. They like to walk around the crib naked. They'll be angry with me if I disrupt their nude expedition. They'll want to wipe me off the face of the earth like the dodo bird." He had a look of disgust as he pictured his dad naked.

"Dodo bird! What does that have to do with anything?" asked Romme.

Chapter 28

Five Thousand G's

"Hm! Nothing! Why am I babbling? Let's smoke some green. You know what, I'll figure out what to do with myself. Congratulations to you and Nia's relationship."

"That's so sweet, thank you, Maleek," complimented Nia.

"Yeah, whatever! You're still bigfoot's sister," replied Maleek.

"I'm not going to insult you back. I know you don't mean that."

"Good, because your breath reeks."

"You'll get used to him. He aggravates everybody. So what's going on with you and Amy?" asked Romme. He paused from breaking down the weed. He stared at Romme with his bottom lip hanging out further than his top lip.

Amy didn't hear anything coming out of her new boyfriend's mouth. Simultaneously she crossed her arms and stared Maleek in the face. Nia looked at Romme, then Maleek. Amy coughed on purpose, clearing her throat, giving her boyfriend a cue to say something about their relationship. She turned her attention to Nia and Romme and then smiled. She cleared her throat again.

"Would you like me to get you a glass of water, or some ginger ale or something?" asked Romme.

"No, thank you," answered Amy as she turned and faced Maleek. She uncrossed her arms and then began plucking his bottom lip with her index finger like a harp. She hummed a tune with her mouth closed while titillating with his bottom lip. Romme and Nia busted out laughing.

"All right, you bully. Quit playing with my lip and I'll tell them," said Maleek.

"Tell us what?" wondered Romme.

"We're boyfriend and girlfriend," revealed Maleek.

"You two will make a great pair," predicted Nia.

"Wow, that's great. You two been knowing each other since kids. That's fantastic," cheered Romme.

"Yeah! I'm going to have to put my boyfriend on the spot if he doesn't speak up. He's embarrassed to be seen with a White woman," said Amy.

"Just because you care for your race doesn't mean that interracial dating is wrong. Love is love," interpreted Nia.

"I'm assuming you won't be harassing me anymore about being pro-Black," foreshadowed Romme.

"Enough about my business. I need to roll this blunt up. Amy, turn the volume on the TV up and flip it to channel 52. DFW's most hilarious videos are coming on in five minutes," said Maleek.

"Yes, you got it, my Mandingo warrior," joked Amy. He looked at her for a few seconds. Nia and Romme were giggling. Just as Maleek finished wrapping the marijuana up in a cigar, DFW's most hilarious videos came on. DFW stood for Dallas-Fort Worth metroplex. He sparked the blunt up. After taking a few puffs, he passed the blunt to Amy. All four of them smoked together while laughing at the videos.

Twenty-seven minutes went by; the blunt was about done. "When they show the last and funniest video, Nia and I need to bounce," informed Romme.

"Why you telling me? You a grown-ass man," responded Maleek. All four of them put their attention on the television show when it came back from the commercial.

"This is your host with the most spokes. Mr. Titty-Ring, we're on our last and most funniest video. Congrats to Troy of Arlington, you're the five-thousand-dollar prize winner. I must say, though, if I was your friend, I'd kick your ass for leaking this video out. Unless you can fight as good as this ruthless sissy in the video. Roll the tape so these folks can see what I'm talking about!"

"Are they talking about the Troy we know?" wondered Romme.

All of a sudden, Romme saw himself on TV. He was bending over while holding his stomach, trying to catch his breath. "Bam!" shouted Titty-Ring as Molly was shown kicking Romme in the ass like a soccer ball. "Let's play that over. Bam!" Shouted the host every time he replayed the video.

"Bam! Bam!"

"That's you, Romme, you're on TV. Why is that woman kicking you in the butt?" asked Amy.

Romme stood up to his feet, enraged. "I'm going to kick Troy's mothafucking ass. That son of a bitch. Let's go, Nia." He marched out the front door; Nia followed him. Maleek busted out in laughter. "She only kicked him in the butt while he was bending over. It's not so bad," said Amy.

Maleek caught his breath to stop laughing. "Titty-Ring keeps replaying that one part. Just wait a second, let him play the whole video. It gets worse." The two of them watched the TV screen closely.

"Bam! Okay, that's enough kickball practice. Let's play it all. Warning to all the people watching at home, this may not be suitable for a younger viewing audience," announced Titty-Ring. He then continued playing the video on TV. Romme was knocked down on the floor, causing him to lie on his belly. Molly jumped on his back and began whaling him with blows to the back of his head.

"Oh my goodness, when did this happen?" asked Amy.

"At the party last night. You were too drunk to remember anything."

"Who's that woman beating on him like that? She fights like Rhonda Rousey."

While chuckling and gasping for air, Maleek had to catch his breath to talk. "That's a man," he mumbled.

Amy had to squint her eyes at the TV screen for a better look. "I'll be a Hershey bar, that is a man." Maleek slumped over on the sofa giggling.

Titty-Ring paused the video. "Before I play the rest of this video, I would like to inform all the folks watching at home about something they may not know. This slender-looking woman is a man. Roll the footage." The video continued. Molly paused while sitting on Romme's back like a jockey. He then applied a choke hold on Romme. Titty-Ring began singing while Romme was being put to sleep. "Silent night! Holy night! All is calm! All is bright! Well, folks, you all know the rest. Thank you for watching. Goodbye until next time. I'm your host with the most spokes, Titty-Ring."

With her mouth wide open, Amy sat there stunned. Maleek's phone started ringing. He glanced at the caller ID. It was Troy calling him. He answered it. "Has Romme seen DFW's *Most Hilarious Videos* today?"

"Yep! Why, what's up?" he answered.

"He called my phone ten times already."

"Pick it up, see what he wants."

"I know what he wants. He wants to beat my ass for leaking that video."

"Split half the money with him, then maybe he won't be mad," Maleek suggested.

Chapter 29

Tracer

"That's a good idea, I'll do that."

"I should get a cut for giving your dumb ass advice. Bye, fool," he said as he hung up the phone.

"Come Tuesday, what will you do about a roof over your head?" asked Amy.

"There's only one option. Move into my parents' house and live like a prisoner. If I do anything illegal, my sambo-ass dad will personally prosecute me."

"How about moving in with me?"

"Your parents are cool, but I can't move into their house when my parents live right next door. That'll be strange."

"Not there, you goofball. I'm moving into my own place tomorrow."

Maleek smiled at her. "You sure that you're ready for us to live together?"

"We've known one another since kids. Why wouldn't I? Plus, I don't want be alone." She leaned over and laid the back of her head on his lap. While looking up, she started chatting with him again. "Can you see yourself with a White woman in the future?" she asked while looking up in his eyes.

"You're the first woman I made love to since I've been out of prison. I'm already with a White woman, one named Amy. A typical name for a White chick," he joked.

"You just stereotyped me. I thought it was supposed to be the other way around."

"I did, huh." He slightly bent over and French-kissed her. "I'm sorry, do you accept my apology?"

"Kiss me again, then I'll forgive you." He pecked her on the lips again. "When's the next time you go to work?" she asked.

"I don't go back to work until Monday."

"Great! We need to arrange our living quarters."

"What's your plan?" he asked.

"What will you do with all your furniture?"

"Everything in here belongs to Romme, except my bed. It's a piece of crap, though. My mattress in prison was more comfortable than the one I own now. I'll drop it off at the landfill."

"Good. All this furniture looks shitty," she implied.

Maleek stared at her. "You ever heard that saying? If you have nothing nice to say, then don't say it. You could've kept that to yourself, buddy, but thanks for being honest."

Amy chuckled a little bit. "You're right, I should've kept that to myself. Ha! You should call Romme and see if we can do all the moving tomorrow morning." He took her advice and called him. They talked on the phone for about five minutes.

He hung up his cell phone. "Romme agreed to your plan. He's not taking anything to Nia's apartment either. Everything here will be going to the landfill."

"Do you mind if I spend the night here with you?" she asked.

"Of course not. Can you handle sleeping on a rough bed?"

Amy had a seductive look in her face. "I'll just lie on you the entire night." He smiled at her. "How did you get so big, Maleek? You're ripped up."

"Lifting weights and doing push-ups my whole prison bid. Working out helped me relieve stress."

"I hate that you had to be in prison, but I like the results. I just thought about something."

"What's that?" he asked.

"I need to stop by my parents' house to get some clothes, along with my toothbrush and other cleaning items. Then after that, I need to go by the Irving Mall to order some furniture."

"Why can't you go to a regular furniture store?" asked Maleek.

"That Cancun Market inside the Irving Mall is the only place that has what I want. Let me guess, you don't want to be seen walking with me."

"Naw! Cancun Market is expensive, that's why I asked." The time now was 1:15 p.m. on a Friday.

Amy jumped up to her feet. "You need to get a new cell phone."

He glanced at his old mobile phone. "It works, that's all that matters."

"Come on, let's hit the road, Chocolate Thunder. We have stuff to do, and I'm warning you right now, Maleek. If you try to hide from me in public, I will hunt you down every time."

He stood up to his feet. "Don't worry, I's won't try to escape, mastah," he replied, imitating a slave.

"You wrong for playing like that," she said while shaking her head.

"You sure right, Vanilla Rain, I shouldn't make fun of my ancestors like that." The two of them exited the apartment. Maleek locked the door behind him. They hopped into Amy's car then began the trip to Irving. Before going to her parents' home, she stopped by a cell phone store. "Why you stop here?" he asked. Amy ignored him. "Cinderella! I know you heard me."

She shut the car door and walked inside the phone store. Maleek opened his door. Before moving, he looked around to see if he knew anybody outside. She was depending on him taking his time to enter the phone store.

"Ha, Amy. How can I help you?" asked Jeff. He was a store employee and an old friend from school.

"Ha, Jeff. Do you remember that special cell phone I was talking about a few days ago?" asked Amy.

"I sure do. You have a cheater that needs to be tracked down?"

"Not exactly. It's complicated. I can't talk about it right now. He'll be coming through that door any second. I don't want him to know about the tracking device."

Maleek entered the building.

"Maleek! What's up, bro? I haven't seen you in a good grip," greeted Jeff.

He walked over to where Jeff and Amy were standing. "What's up, Jeff? I thought you worked in the air condition field."

"I do, bro. I got a part-time job because I need the extra money."

"Well damn! You making at least thirty to forty dollars an hour. What are you doing? Building an underground fortress for the apocalypse?"

"I have eight kids, bro. You know how us Mexicans and Blacks do. Our kids want Air Jordans, Polo, and Prada."

"Goddamn! Mexicans be fucking like rabbits. When y'all have children, it be big-ass litters. Wear a condom every once in a while. You really have eight kids?"

"Yep," answered Jeff.

"Let me find out that you out there tricking."

"Hell naw, I'm not. My wife would stab me in my sleep. Either that, or my child support would leave me broke."

"Man! If you had to pay child support, you'd be paying two separate mortgages, plus utilities."

Jeff's smile turned into a frown. "That's real funny, Mr. Comedian. It was good seeing you two again. I better get back to work." He handed Amy the phone that she had planned on getting ahead of time.

Chapter 30

Ruffneck

She took it to the front register to have it activated. After buying it, she spun around to exit the store. She gave it to Maleek. "That's yours, baby."

He held it in his hand as he glanced at it. "Amy! You didn't have to get me a phone. I already own one," he too explained her as he trailed her out of the building.

They hopped into the car. "It's no big deal. I got it for free. It came with my contract plan. It can be our new relationship phone. You need to transfer all your contact information to your new phone, then get rid of your old phone. There are no secrets in our relationship," she said while cheesing.

While she was driving off, he tucked his upper lip in, leaving the bottom lip poking out further. He stared at her smiling from ear to ear, wondering what she was up to. After a minute of being suspicious, he began playing with his new phone. "It comes with a zoom-in camera and Internet access," informed Amy.

"Thank you, it's nice, but what's the reason you gave it to me?"

"Reason? There's no reason at all. I told you it was free with my plan. I don't need two phones, so I figured I'd give it to somebody. Why not my new boyfriend?"

He started thinking, rubbing his chin. "That makes sense, but my gut feeling tells me that you're up to something." With his bottom lip hanging out, his eyes became narrow as he stared at Amy.

She took her attention off the road for a second to peek at Maleek, then put her sights back on the road. "You look so funny when you hang your lip out like that. You remind me of Mushmouth off of *Fat Albert*," she said as she began laughing.

He looked in the rearview mirror, then untucked his lip. "You got jokes, huh? I would've never thought that White people watched that cartoon."

"I bet you never thought Bill Cosby would buy a Mickey from a drug dealer neither. Those poor ladies woke up and seen their drawers down to their ankles. First thing they probably said was, 'This mothafucker done stole my pudding.'"

"You know he got out of prison on appeal," Maleek informed her as he quickly turned his attention to her. With a grin on his face, he exploded laughing. "You're still smart and funny. You haven't changed since high school."

"Thank you, that's so sweet of you to say that."

"Yeah, maybe you're a little too smart for your own good."

"What's that supposed to mean?"

"Don't think that I forgot about this mobile phone. I don't know your plot right now, so you're still a suspect. Just know this, though, I got my eyes on you, Hillary Clinton."

Amy giggled hard. "You feel I'm conducting a cell phone scandal, huh? Do you have evidence of this accusation, Dick Tracey?"

He had no answer for her question; he crossed his arms. Amy parked in front of her parents' house. The time now was 2:03 p.m. on a Friday. "Help me with my suitcases," said Amy. He followed her inside her parents' house. While exiting the house with her first load of luggage, her parents had already parked in the driveway.

Alice and Todd exited their vehicle and approached Maleek and Amy. Her parents greeted Maleek with a tight hug. He felt strange, yet loved also.

"What's going on with you two bumblebees?" asked Alice.

"I'm getting all my clothes and other small stuff ready for my apartment tomorrow," answered Amy.

"Why would you stay in a hotel when you could just stay home for one more night, honey?"

"I'll be moving into my new place from Maleek's apartment in Arlington."

"Is there something we should know?" asked Todd.

Amy smiled. "Maleek and I are boyfriend and girlfriend."

"That's great, honey," said Todd and Alice simultaneously.

"When's the engagement?" asked Alice.

"It's a little early to ask that question, Mom," responded Amy.

Chapter 31

You a Man Now

"How is life treating you, Maleek, you all right?" asked Todd.

"I'm doing good. I can't complain, sir," replied Maleek.

Todd reached over and grabbed Maleek by the shoulder, then squeezed firmly. "Just call me Pops from now on, son."

You must be joking, thought Maleek in his head. "Yes, sir. I mean, you got it, Pops."

"How'd you get so big?" asked Alice.

"Yeah, you are pretty big. I swear I felt some shoulder pads under that shirt," Todd said in agreement with his wife.

"During my bid in prison, I basically lived out on the weight pile," explained Maleek.

"I'm certain that Amy will stay safe with you," assured Alice.

Todd started rapping. "My little girl got a ruffneck. Got to have a ruffneck, she wanna ruffneck."

"Dad! Stop it," demanded Amy.

"What! I'm just singing MC Lyte's song."

Maleek giggled.

"Don't encourage him, Maleek," demanded Amy.

"Well, we better let you two kiddos finish moving. Come on, Vanilla Ice, we need to get these groceries out of the car," ordered Alice. They began taking their edibles inside the house.

Once done carrying their groceries inside, her parents went back into the house, leaving the door open for Amy. Amy carried a small bag as Maleek trailed behind her carrying a suitcase. She exited the house, then stepped to the side and paused to shut the front door behind him. Just as he was about to step out of the house, "Amy! How are you, darling?" shouted Momma D from next door. Daloris was leaving the house. Maleek heard her voice. He blocked his head with the suitcase to keep from being seen.

Amy closed the front door as he walked out of her parents' house. "Ha, Momma D! I'm doing fine, how are you doing?"

"I'm just peachy, baby girl. I'm on my way to the drugstore." She had seen a guy walking out of Amy's house, but she couldn't see his face. "Who's the man carrying the suitcase?" Amy turned to look at Maleek. She saw him hiding his face with the suitcase while walking to her car. Just as he went to grab the door handle to get in the vehicle, she pressed the automatic lock on her key chain, locking her car doors.

When his attempt to get into the automobile failed, he stood there in silence, holding the travel case up high by his shoulder like a waiter toting a dish tray. Amy trotted over to him; she tried snatching the suitcase from behind him, initiating a tug-of-war with him. Using one hand, she struggled tremendously, like the wrong person trying to pull King Arthur's sword out the stone. She then gripped the bag with two hands and lifted her leg up, placing her foot in his back for leverage. They both were grunting while tugging back and forth. "Give it up," shouted Amy.

What is wrong with these young people nowadays? thought Momma D in her mind.

Finally, she yanked the suitcase from him. Her backward momentum caused her to fall on her ass. "Huh!" she groaned as she hit the ground. Maleek extended his arm to help her up. She rose up to her feet then dusted her butt off.

"Maleek! Boy, what are you doing over there?" shouted Momma D. Amy spun around to face her.

"Please don't refer to me as a boy, Mom."

"Boy! If you don't answer me, I'll come over there and suplex your ass."

"I'm helping Amy with her luggage. She's moving," he answered. "Huh!" he grunted as Amy elbowed him in the gut.

"Oh," retorted Momma D. She then started walking toward her car. Amy raised her elbow up to sock Maleek in the stomach again.

"Tell her about our relationship," she ordered under her breath.

"Okay, wait, I'll tell her," said Maleek, yielding. Amy lowered her elbow. "Mom!"

Momma D came to a standstill. "What, boy?"

"I have something to tell you."

"I'm listening."

"Amy and I are dating."

A wide grin appeared on Momma D's face. She walked over to the new couple and gave Amy a tight hug. "Now you are becoming a man. I guess I should stop calling you a boy. You got you a good girl too. It's about time. I was starting to assume you're a faggot. When will I get some grandbabies?"

His mother was embarrassing him. "Mom! We'll talk about that stuff later. We need to go."

Momma D pinched his cheekbone and tugged on it. "I'm so proud of you, son. You two will make some pretty little mulattos."

"Thank you for your compliment, Momma D," replied Amy as she started crying. They hugged again.

Momma D pulled out a business card of her dentistry, then handed it to Amy. "Keep that, baby, so when those grandkids are ready, Momma D gone make sure their teeth are taken care of."

Maleek rolled his eyes in frustration. "I didn't know you were a fortune teller. Tell me, once our children come into your dental office, will the service be free, or will you charge us, Mother Cleo?"

Her smile flipped upside down like a tornado appearing out of nowhere on a beautiful day. "Who are you talking to with those slick-ass catfish lips? You better be thankful that I'm happy for Amy right now. Otherwise, I'd climb up on the roof of that automobile, then jump off and drop-kick your ass. Give me another hug, Amy. Make sure you call me Momma from now on. Well, I better get to this drugstore." They unlocked hugs.

Momma D went to her vehicle and drove away. Maleek and Amy hopped into her car. "Where we headed now?" he asked.

"I need to stop by the Irving Mall to order some furniture from Cancun Market. Then we'll head to your apartment." Amy drove off to the mall.

Chapter 32

Hustled

It was two thirty on the dot when they parked in the mall parking lot. Before they could even exit the car, he was peeping around like a paranoid drug dealer on the run from the FBI.

Amy gazed at him. "You okay?"

"Yeah! Why are you asking?"

"You seem a little uneasy."

"Naw, sugar tank, I'm good."

"Cool! Let's go." Amy stepped out of the car. Maleek also exited the car. They met up by the trunk of the vehicle. When they started walking toward the entrance, Amy grabbed his hand and held it. The inlet of the mall they entered in was the food court. More people will be there at once, more than any other part of the shopping center. Not even a minute went by before he recognized some people they knew. It was Tinna and Brad, old high school buddies. Another interracial couple; Tinna was Black, Brad White. Amy hadn't noticed them yet, but Maleek had. His first thought was their interaction at Mr. Yumburger. The two couples were approximately twenty feet in front of one another. Bound to cross paths if they kept walking.

Maleek swiftly scooted over, yanking Amy along with him. They came to a standstill in front of an electronic board. "You damn near pulled my arm out of my socket," fussed Amy.

"I saw something on this billboard. Watch it with me," replied Maleek. The electric board stood about ten feet, four feet wide.

Different advertisements took turns appearing on the board. She began watching it with him. After a minute of viewing the electric display panel, they kept looking at the same exhibits. He poked his head around the right corner of the board. Tinna and Brad had stopped by a smoothie shop. *Fuck*, cursed Maleek in his head. He knew he couldn't hold Amy here for long. He was counting on Brad and Tinna passing them up by now.

Amy looked at him, then the advertisement panel. She was suspicious but knew he was trying to hide their relationship from somebody.

"Why are we still standing here like a caveman seeing fire for the first time? The same stuff is showing over and over." Brad and Tinna had begun walking their way when she was asking that question.

Maleek focused his attention back on the electric board. "Look! There's more coming up," he responded.

She continued observing it again just as Tinna and Brad where about to walk past them. "You been sniffing paint or something? Nothing new is being shown."

While the couple was passing by, Tinna recognized her old friend's voice. "Amy!" she shouted as she stopped to look in their direction.

Amy turned to where she heard someone calling her name. A huge grin appeared on her face. "Tinna," she shouted as she darted toward her old friend. She hugged her tightly, then she also hugged Brad. "Good God, it's been a long time since I've seen you two. You two have been dating since high school. I can't believe you two are still a couple."

Tinna held up her left hand to show her wedding ring. "Look, girl!"

"Huh!" mumbled Amy with her mouth wide open. She and Tinna hugged again. "What brings y'all here? What are my long-lost friends shopping for?"

"I dragged Brad here to the Irving Mall because I wanted to order some furniture from Cancun Market."

"What! Get out of here, girl. That's the same reason why we came up here."

Brad gave her a crazy look. "Who's we?"

"Me and..." Amy glanced to her left and right. Maleek had disappeared like a ninja. "He was just right here next to me, my boyfriend."

"Do we know him?" asked Tinna.

"Yeah! You remember Maleek, right?"

"Maleek! You two are dating? Wow! That's a shocker. He said some mean words about Tinna and I being together. It confused me because I know he isn't racist. Plus, he's the one who introduced me and Tinna," explained Brad.

"Our relationship just began today. He's a work in progress. When I came back to town from college, I saw firsthand how his attitude was. We all know Maleek from high school. Clearly, he's not the same sweet person we used to know. Prison has had a serious mental effect on him, but he's coming around. I tell you two what. Walk with me to go find him."

"It could take an hour to find him, Amy. Especially when he can vanish like Houdini," replied Tinna.

Amy pulled out her cell phone with a smirk on her face. "Not even a magician can hide from technology."

"What makes you say that?" wondered Brad.

"I have a tracking device on Maleek's mobile phone. He doesn't know, so please don't tell him when we find him."

"Oh! Amy, you are slicker than hair grease, girl," said Tinna.

"Thanks, girl. Do you see this little blue dot blinking on my cell phone screen?"

"Yes," answered Tinna and Brad at the same time.

"Well, that's our beloved boy blue Maleek. Let's start the hunt for our fugitive," she announced like a warden. They began the search.

While hiding in the arcade room, Maleek figured he'd play some arcade games. He only had four quarters; he'd just used two. He selected *Mortal Combat*. After a couple of minutes playing the game, he reached the last stage. Before he could play, though, a little kid tapped him on his hip.

"Ha there, little bugger," greeted Maleek.

"May I have fifty cents?" replied the little kid.

"Yeah, why not. I don't need it anymore." He reached into his pants pocket and gave his two last quarters to the little boy. The youngster barely stood four feet. He watched Maleek battle against the last boss on *Mortal Combat*. He won the first round. Just as he was about to beat the whole game, the little kid put his change into the same arcade box. Then he pressed *start*.

"Little bugger! Why'd you go and do that? I was about to beat the game." With no reply, the youngster held on to the joystick while staring at him, then he started blinking his eyes a lot. "You just took the last of my change, but now you can't talk. You just gone stare at me and blink your eyes, huh? You got Parkinson's disease or something? All right, I'm cool with the silent treatment. When I beat yo little butt off the arcade, don't go crying to your momma."

The kid's head was barely high enough to see over the control panel. "You wanna stand on my foot before this ass-whoopin' begins? Maybe you can see the screen better." The youngster looked at him and blinked his eyes. The match had begun between them. Maleek won the first round; the kid won the second round. Only one round was left to determine the winner.

"Damn! You actually know how to play. No more Mr. Nice Guy, say bye-bye," teased Maleek. The little boy beat him in ten seconds. "You little panhandler, you took my last quarters, then knocked me off the game. You're a con artist." *Finish him*, shouted the arcade box. The little kid started pressing buttons fast. All of a sudden, the screen got dark. "Ah!" screamed Maleek's character. *Fatality*, announced the arcade game.

Amy, followed by Tinna and Brad, approached Maleek. "Why you mean-mugging this little kid?" asked Amy.

Chapter 33

That Will Burn

Maleek turned around to face her. "This little son of a goat took the last of my change and beat me off the game. Then to throw salt on the wound, he chopped off my character's head. Now he can't speak all of a sudden."

The little boy turned around. "My momma told me not to talk to strangers." He then continued to play the arcade game.

"Did your momma also tell you not to hustle people?" replied Maleek.

"Whatever, loser," responded the kid. Tinna and Brad were laughing.

Maleek started taking off his belt. "Why you little!" Amy grabbed him by the elbow and dragged him out of the arcade.

"Take it easy, bro, he's just a kid," said Brad.

"Bro! Who are you calling—?" Maleek stopped talking because Amy was staring at him with her arms crossed. She appeared to be upset.

"Why were you so mean to them when they saw you on Thanksgiving?" asked Amy.

"Okay, look, you two. I shouldn't have said what I did. Please accept my apology," pleaded Maleek. They both forgave him. Brad went to hug him; Maleek smashed his hand into his face, stopping him. It looked like Brad had run into a clothing line as he bent back-

EMBARRASSED TO BE WITH AMY

ward in a strange motion. It seemed like he was doing the limbo. "I don't need no hug from a man. Plus I'm not no damn Care Bear."

"Oh! Sorry about that," replied Brad as he stood up straight.

"What happened to you, Maleek? I've never seen you so angry before," asked Tinna.

"When I came out of prison, it scarred me mentally, turned me to stone, and left me bitter. It really made me despise White people. Deep down in my soul, I know all White people aren't the same. Now that I'm with Amy, I'm trying my hardest not to be resentful," explained Maleek.

Amy hugged him, then kissed him. "Come on, everybody, we'll chat later. Let's go order some furniture." All four of them walked to Cancun Market together. After selecting all her household goods, Amy paid for the home furnishings, along with the delivery cost. The two couples had parked in the same parking lot, so they walked together to leave.

"How did you find me, Amy?" asked Maleek.

Amy looked him in the eyes. "I sniffed the turkey bacon grease smell that you left behind." Amy, Brad, and Tinna began giggling.

Maleek's bottom lip poked out as he got suspicious. "That's very funny, Monica Lewinsky, but I did not have sexual relationships with that jive turkey." Brad and Tinna couldn't stop laughing. Amy put a frown on her face after hearing what her boyfriend had just said.

"You better watch those lips, Mushmouth," warned Amy.

Before the two couples parted ways, they exchanged phone numbers. Amy drove west on Highway 183 toward Arlington. "What time will the furniture be delivered tomorrow?" asked Maleek.

"Twelve thirty p.m.," she replied.

"What about a refrigerator?"

"One comes with the apartment."

"What about a dryer and washing machine?"

"I've already ordered them from Rent-A-Center. They'll be delivered to the apartment at three," answered Amy.

"I see you plan early and stay ready."

She glanced at him for a few seconds. "If you only knew." She then put her eyes back on the road.

He looked at her and poked his bottom lip out. "What's that supposed to mean?"

"Nothing, my chicken and dumplings."

Maleek was still staring at her. "Chicken and dumplings, huh! I've been knowing you my whole life. I know when you're up to something. I got my eyes on you."

"You got your eyes on me, hm! Are you imagining me naked?" she asked in a seductive voice.

He licked his lips. "Hm! Baby, I wanna cover you with some mashed potatoes, then pour some brown gravy on you. Then eat it off."

Amy had a crazy look on her face. "Are you insane? The mashed potatoes and gravy would burn me. Most people would use whipped cream with peaches, cherries, or strawberries. You mentioned a side dish, a steamy hot one at that. You could have at least said coleslaw, something that wouldn't hurt."

"I was thinking outside the box, you know. Something different from the ordinary. Coleslaw is nasty to me. Also, it's cold."

"When you were thinking, what box were you looking at? A Kentucky fried chicken ten-piece?" He laughed at her comment. The time was 3:46 p.m. when they drove into Maleek's apartment complex. When they entered the apartment, Romme and Nia were sitting on the couch. The TV and the lights were cut off. It was completely dark in the living room.

Before Maleek shut the door behind him, he looked around the shadowy apartment. "What in the jack-o'-lantern is you two doing in here? Y'all playing with a Ouija board?" he wondered while switching on the lights.

"I got a rental truck for tomorrow," said Romme.

"Why didn't you wait? I could've paid half of the rental fee," replied Maleek.

"Don't worry about it. I collected 2,500 dollars from Troy. I should've kicked his ass, then taken all the money."

"It's not that big of a deal. Plus you got half the money."

"Everybody on Facebook and Twitter keeps making fun of me. To make it worse, that video has the most hits on YouTube. I can't believe this shit," complained Romme.

"Don't sweat it, you were drunk, baby," comforted Nia.

"Bullsh—!" blurted Maleek, pretending to sneeze.

Chapter 34

Bragging

"Man! Fuck you, Maleek," cursed Romme.

"What? I just sneezed," he replied.

"At least you're not in high school or college. You don't have to encounter people you know," sympathized Amy.

"Thanks, Amy, but tell that to my parents. First my momma called me. She ordered me to go get a rematch. My pops called me next. He cursed me out. He complained that I made our last name look bad. All the guys at his job's been clowning him because his son got beat up by a sissy."

"It's not the end of the world, bro. Plus you have 2,500 dollars in your pocket. You got a new girlfriend you're moving in with. Your good," insisted Maleek.

"Yeah! You're right, man, I'm good," he agreed.

"Well, Daniel-san. I would like to pep your ego up some more, but I'm tired. I'm a take a nap. I didn't get no sleep yesterday. I was too busy talking to a naked dodo bird and hiding from White people."

"Do what?" said Nia.

"Please! Don't ask. It's a long story," responded Maleek as he walked to his room. Amy trailed behind him. They closed the room door behind them. He quickly lay in his bed, facedown in the pillow.

"I forgot my luggage in the car," remembered Amy.

"Just leave your bags in the car. We're moving into your apartment tomorrow anyways. All you need is an outfit to change into tomorrow, along with your toothbrush," said Maleek. She walked out of his room, then exited the apartment. She grabbed some clothes, along with a toothbrush and bathing supplies.

After getting the supplies she needed, she made a beeline to Maleek's room. They both went to sleep in the middle of the afternoon. Somebody knocked on Maleek's door. He woke up. "Come in," he shouted. Romme poked his head through the crack of the door.

"I need to go get the U-Haul truck at seven in the morning. Will you drive me up to the rental office to pick it up?" asked Romme.

Maleek lifted his head off the pillow. "Yeah! Call Troy and ask him if he'll help us move."

"Troy and Amanda will be too busy packing their stuff up tomorrow. They're moving into a house. They even bought a puppy for their new home."

"We're all separating and moving in with spouses."

"We're not young anymore, cuz, we're all grown up. We'll all stay in touch."

Maleek looked at his window. It was dark outside. "What time is it?" he wondered.

"It's 11:12 p.m.," Romme answered.

"Damn! Time went by fast. I'm still tired, though."

"Amy must've worn your ass out, huh!" When he heard Romme make that comment, Maleek looked down at Amy's face; the back of her head was facing Romme. Her eyes were closed. He assumed she was still sleep.

He gazed back at Romme. "Man, please, I tore that." He got quiet instantly and then looked down at Amy's face again. She had one eye open, staring directly at him. "What were you saying?" asked Romme.

"I said, man, I must have been snoring."

"Oh! Well, I'll see you in the morning," he said while closing the room door.

"Wait," Maleek shouted.

"What's up?" Romme said, pausing in the doorway.

"Out of me, you, and Troy, I wonder who'll have kids first?"

"I don't know, but I'm excited to have kids. See you tomorrow, bro." Romme closed the door. Maleek laid the back of his head on the pillow; Amy laid her head on top of his chest.

"I love you," she said.

"I love you too," he replied. They went back to sleep. He opened his eyes. It was 6:00 a.m. on a Saturday.

Chapter 35

Proud

Before he could rise out of bed, his cell phone started ringing. He answered it. "Maleek! What are you doing?" asked his dad.

He was surprised that his father was calling him. He figured his pops was trying to catch him doing something illegal. "What do you want? Whatever it is, I didn't do it."

"Boy, hush up. If I wanted to, I'd plant something on your Black ass, then throw you in prison faster than a Black man accused of raping a White lady. I need you to come over right away."

"For what? I have stuff to do, Eric Holder."

"Boy! You done lost your gopher ass mind talking to me like that. I'm still your father. You pot-smoking, clunker-cruising, fairy-tale, burger-crafting shit wipe. Get your sticky-fingers, werewolf-looking ass over here as soon as you can. I have something important to give to you."

"All right, Ben Carson, I'll be there as soon as I can."

"Hurry up, son, I have business to handle," said Tyrone. He hung up, ending the call. *Damn! Why does everybody make fun of me flipping burgers? That's all they can come up with to insult me*, he thought in his head. He gently lifted Amy's head off his chest onto the pillow.

"Where are you going?" asked Amy.

"Before Romme and I go and pick up the U-Haul truck, I need to stop by my parents' house. I must leave early to pick up the truck on time," he explained. He walked into the restroom to brush his teeth. When he was done, he walked toward his room door and opened it to leave. He came to a standstill in the middle of the doorway. "Be ready to go when we get back," he said.

"Okay," she replied.

He went straight to Romme's room and knocked on the door. Romme came out of his room fully dressed. "What's up?" he asked as he closed the door behind him.

"We need to leave earlier than planned. I need to stop by my parents' house first," explained Maleek.

"Cool, I'm ready now."

"Don't you want to at least brush your teeth?"

"I already did."

"I can't tell. It smells like a dead possum that's been lying on the road for three days. You been eating Nia's pussy?"

"Go to hell, Maleek!" shouted Nia through the door.

"Ladies first," he replied.

"If we're going to continue our friendship, you need to respect my woman," suggested Romme.

"All right, bro, my bad. Come on, let's ride out," he said as the two of them exited the front door.

The two of them hopped into Maleek's car. The time was 6:12 a.m. when they began the drive to Irving. He needed to stop by his parents' house first. He was clueless as to why his dad wanted him to come by now. What was so important that his pops had to give him? While cruising on Highway 360, on the way to Irving, he couldn't stop thinking about what awaited him.

"What's the reason for stopping by your parents' house?" asked Romme.

"I don't know. My dad informed me that he had something important to give me. He wanted me to pick it up now," answered Maleek.

"What is it?"

"I don't know and didn't ask." While watching the road ahead of him, he pondered on what it could be. He was baffled like a kid taking an SAT test and didn't study. The two of them kept quiet during the rest of the trip to Irving.

When they parked in front of Maleek's parents' house, the time was 6:37 a.m. Maleek stepped out of his car. Before shutting the door behind him, he told Romme to wait in the vehicle. He closed the door and then began walking toward the house. He made it halfway to the door when Tyrone exited the front door. His dad had a tuxedo on.

The two of them met up on the sidewalk trail that led to the porch. Without saying a word, his father pulled a small box out of his pocket. It was covered in wrapping paper. He handed it to his son, then started walking to his automobile. Tyrone opened his driver's side door. Before getting in the car, he stared at Maleek. "I love you, son, and I'm proud of you." He hopped into his vehicle, then drove away. Maleek hadn't heard anything positive about himself from his dad's mouth ever since he got out of prison. He jumped back into his car.

"What is it?" asked Romme.

"How can I know? You still see the wrapping paper on it," replied Maleek. He set the small present on the dashboard, then sat back in his seat and stared out the front windshield. He was stunned and confused. He was contemplating why his dad told him he was proud of him.

"What's wrong, bro?"

"My pops told me he was proud of me when he handed me that box. Proud of what? What have I done? He hasn't said nothing good to me since I got out of prison."

"What if he's trying to trick you? There could be a recording device in there. He might be trying to put you back in prison."

Maleek's bottom lip was hanging out further than his top lip as he gave Romme a dumbfounded look. "You must have a marshmallow for a brain. Not a s'more, just a marshmallow. You make it seem like I'm a kingpin or something. I'm driving a Pinto for crying out loud." He snatched the box off the dashboard, then quickly tore off the wrapping paper. It was a jewelry box. He opened it. Inside was an engagement ring, included with a wedding band.

"Damn! Those are platinum rings with princess-cut diamonds. You're looking at a few hundred thousand dollars or more in that box."

"Why would he give me this?"

"It's because of Amy. He's proud of you and her being a couple," figured Romme.

"I don't understand."

"Amy's a college graduate. Your parents know and love her. They're starting to respect you because of her. Apparently in their minds, they believe you're becoming a real man by being with her. They want you to marry her."

Maleek rubbed his chin, then gazed at Romme. "You know what, Steve Wilkos, you're freakin' right." Romme smiled at him. "I really love her, but I'm embarrassed to be seen with Amy."

"You're a fucking imbecile. Forget that mentality. You need to drop that pro-Black attitude. You can still be for your people, but love is love. Think about it, Frederick Douglass had a White girl. You two were meant to be, bro. God doesn't care about your skin tone. Plus, Amy is fine. She has hips like a Black woman."

Maleek started up his car engine. "You're right, cuz, I need to get a grip on myself. I know one thing, you better stop eyeballing my woman."

While Maleek began to drive off, Romme held his hands in the air as if somebody had pointed a gun at him, then cheesed. "Ha, I only mentioned that so you would come to your senses."

They now were headed to a rental truck office in Arlington. It was 7:13 a.m. when they arrived at the rental truck place. Maleek continued to drive his car while Romme drove the U-Haul truck. They pulled into the apartment parking lot at 7:30 a.m. on the dot. Romme parked the truck in backward, directly in front of their apartment door.

Chapter 36

Roadkill

The two of them exited the vehicle, then went inside. Nia and Amy were sitting on the living room sofa. "We all ready to go?" asked Nia as she stood up.

"Since everything is going to the landfill, Romme and I will handle all the moving. You two can go home. We'll meet up later once we're done," replied Maleek.

"Wouldn't it be quicker if we helped?"

"Look here, Wonder Woman. I know you're stronger than the two of us combined because your ancestry is from the Mothman. I'm pretty sure we two can manage, though. By the way, you've done a great job of hiding your moth wings."

Nia placed her hands on her hips as she leaned to her left. "I hope you pick up something heavy and slip a disk out of your vertebrae. You slimy, shell-hiding snail. I should throw some salt on your punk ass to watch you shrivel up." After dissing Maleek, she gave Romme a hug, then walked out the front door. After hugging Maleek, Amy trailed behind her.

Romme stared at him. "What happened to respecting my lady?" he asked.

"I'm sorry! I couldn't help it. That's my last insult. You have my word," responded Maleek. They began moving everything out of the apartment into the U-Haul truck. The time was 8:20 a.m. when they loaded up the truck.

They both hopped into the truck, and Romme drove while Maleek sat in the passenger seat. Romme took off from the parking space on the way out of the apartment complex, headed to the landfill.

"Stop!" shouted Maleek. As Romme slammed on the brakes, the heavy U-Haul truck made a loud screeching noise.

"What the fuck, man!" fussed Romme.

"There's a puppy in the road." The little puppy began barking at the truck.

Romme put his head closer to the windshield to get a better look at the puppy. "Well, I'll be a chocolate chip cookie."

"Why you say that? You got a taste for some cookies?"

"That's Troy's puppy."

"Thanks for stopping! Here I come! Get over here, Fluffy!" shouted Troy as he started walking toward the street. He hadn't spotted the guys in the truck. His attention was focused on Fluffy.

Out of the blue, Romme had a demented look on his face. He stomped on the gas pedal before Troy could make it to Fluffy. "Wait! Stop!" yelled Troy.

"Arh!" whimpered the puppy that was now under the huge wheel of the U-Haul truck.

With his mouth wide open in shock, Maleek slowly turned his head to look Romme in the eyes.

"You murderer!" Romme's laugh sounded like a serial killer clown.

"Back it up," yelled Troy as he kept pounding on the front bumper of the truck.

Amanda came running out of the apartment. "Where's Fluffy? Is he okay?"

"I'm looking for him now," he responded as the U-Haul truck backed up in reverse. "I don't see him."

"Aaah!" screamed Amanda at the top of her lungs.

"What! What is it?" he reacted. She pointed at the right front tire. Fluffy was sticking to the wheel like a crushed bug. Blood and guts were sticking to the tire like a flat sloppily made pancake. Troy stepped backward to get a view through the front windshield. He saw the white teeth of Romme grinning. "Motherfucker!"

Troy ran to the driver-side door. He hopped on the ledge and tried to get in the truck. Romme had the door locked already. Amanda ran back into the apartment crying loudly. "You better jump down before I take off," warned Romme.

"I'm going to beat yo ass, fool," responded Troy while jerking back on the door handle. Romme started to drive off toward the exit gate of the apartment complex. While waiting for the gate to open all the way up, Romme was nonchalantly whistling "When Johnny Comes Marching Home," simultaneously ignoring Troy hanging on to the door and beating on the window with his free hand.

Troy looked like a one-man rioter as he beat up on the truck. Maleek's lungs were hurting from laughing too hard.

When the gate was completely open, Romme accelerated toward the busy intersection and stopped to look both ways. Troy began to get scared when he saw the truck headed for the main road. "Okay! Wait! I'm jumping off right now."

"You have three seconds," retorted Romme. Troy slowly spun around to jump off. Romme quickly rolled down his window, then grabbed and held on tightly to the back of Troy's robe. When he jumped off the stepladder of the truck, his thin robe ripped from his sleeves. He rolled on the ground nude; only his biceps and triceps were covered. They could see Troy in the rearview mirror running butt naked toward his apartment.

"You wrong for that," Maleek let it be known.

"Now we're even for him putting that tape on TV," replied Romme. He drove off on the way to the landfill. After emptying the furniture out of the U-Haul, they made it back to the apartment at 9:30 a.m. "Nia will pick me up at the rental truck office."

"Well, I'll see you around, bro." The two of them dapped hands, then hugged. Romme drove off first. Maleek had the address to Amy's new apartment on him. He knew exactly where it was at; he was familiar with Arlington. Before driving off, he gazed at the engagement ring. He began the trip to his new home. It was 9:47

a.m. when he arrived at his new residence. He put the jewelry box in his pocket, then walked up to the door.

Before he could knock, Amy opened it up. He walked in; they began kissing. While kissing, he shut the door behind him. After finding the apartment, he went back outside to bring his luggage inside.

Chapter 37

Love of My Life

"Come with me to Kroger. We need to buy some groceries," said Amy.

"Let me take a shower first. Romme took all the towels and washrags from the apartment. Do you have some in your luggage?" asked Maleek.

"Yes, I've already unpacked everything. Look in the pantry." He went to the restroom to take a shower. Once he was done getting dressed, he placed the ring in his back pocket. The two of them exited the apartment and hopped into Amy's car. They were now on the way to Kroger.

They pulled into the Kroger parking lot and parked. He exited the vehicle faster than her. Once she stepped out of the car, she began walking toward the passenger door. Maleek was nowhere to be found. She looked inside, but she knew he wasn't in the car. *No way could he disappear that fast*, she thought. She pulled out her cell phone to observe the tracking device. The blinking dot representing Maleek was indicating him to be on the back side of the car.

"Baby, what are you doing?" she asked as she walked around the trunk of the car and found him.

Maleek looked up at her. He was kneeling down on one knee. "I'm lacing up my shoes. I thought you'd seen me," he responded. She stood there waiting on him. "Go ahead, baby, I'll catch up with you."

"Okay," she replied. While glancing at her cell phone, she walked off laughing. "You can run, but you can't hide," she whispered to herself. Watching her cell phone screen, she saw the blinking dot moving in a wide circle. It was headed toward the other entrance on the left side of the store. *The milkman is on the move*, she thought to herself. She grabbed a shopping cart, then began shopping. She didn't wait for him; she already knew where he was.

Once she made it to the meat section, she called Maleek on his cell phone. He answered it. "What do you want for dinner tonight?" asked Amy.

"I'll let you pick," he responded.

"I was thinking pork chops."

"I don't eat Porky the Pig."

"Why not? Does it have anything to do with the cartoon character? You must really like him."

"You must have forgotten that I'm Muslim."

"I actually did forget. I guess we need to sit down and talk about us. What do you feel like eating tonight?"

"How about some steaks?" figured Maleek.

"That's cool. Meet me by the meat department. That way, we can shop together."

"I'm on my way now," he said as he headed to the meat department. He had seen somebody who used to be in prison with him.

It was Hanif, the prison imam during the time Maleek was locked up. Hanif was a big influence on his outward look of the world. If he saw his old friend with a White woman, he would be very disappointed.

Maleek hid around the corner of the chip aisle. He moved in a fast pace to the meat department, meeting up with Amy. "I suggest you stay with me because I don't know what you like." He started tossing all kinds of meats in the cart. "Why are you rushing?" she asked.

"I'm not Russian, I'm Black. You must think I'm a spy." She gave him a stern look. "I'm just excited about our new home. Shouldn't we hurry up before the furniture gets there?"

"It's only 10:30 a.m. We have until twelve thirty before the home furnishings arrive at the apartment."

He heard Hanif talking on his phone. He was coming around the corner of another aisle, moving closer to them.

He took off marching to another aisle. "Don't make me hunt you down," she threatened. She started chasing him with the shopping cart. He glanced back over his shoulder; he saw her pursuing him. She had a huge grin on her face. He sped up toward the front of the store.

Before he had made it to the end of the aisle, she halted just as he made a left and went to the next aisle. She gazed at her cell phone's tracking app. She knew he was on the next aisle, moving in her direction. She quickly spun around and waited on the end of the aisle.

Maleek began to jog a little; he didn't know that Amy was waiting on him. When he came around the corner, he spotted Amy to his left. *How could she catch up with me so quick? It seems like a scary movie. No matter how fast I run, she walks and catches me*, he thought in his mind. He bolted off down the next aisle, running back toward the front registers. Amy acted like she was following behind him on the same aisle when she saw him looking back.

He made a left up the next aisle, now moving back to where he had just come from. Viewing her phone, she knew he was backtracking. She quickly turned around and waited at the end of the aisle at the back of the store. "No running, sir," shouted an employee when he was approaching the end of the lane. He looked back over his shoulder.

"Huh!" he muttered. He was tripped by somebody. He hit the ground and slid a few yards. Once he stopped sliding, his head was poking out the passageway. There stood Amy to his left. Hanif had seen him sliding on the tile like he was trying to make it to home base.

Maleek peeped behind him while stretched out on the floor. "Why you little quarter-stealing leprechaun." It was the kid who had swindled him for his change then beat him off the arcade game at the mall. The kid took off running while giggling.

"Maleek, is that you? Are you okay?" asked Hanif.

"Sweetie, you can't hide from me," said Amy.

"Sweetie! You're dating this she-devil. After all the knowledge you gained while we were locked up. What's wrong with you, brother?" asked Hanif.

"Watch what you say about my woman. I'll beat yo muthafucking ass. Besides, there's no room for racism in Islam," responded Maleek. She smiled on hearing her man's comment.

"You just gone sell out, huh!" replied Hanif.

Maleek sat up but stayed down on one knee. "I don't give a Doberman pincher's booty hole about what you think of me. I haven't sold out, but if you don't get yo doodoo-brown-looking ass stepping, I'll beat yo ass so bad, God himself will cover his eyes while I'm kicking your ass." Hanif started walking away fast.

"Get off the floor, Maleek," ordered Amy.

He scooted closer to her. "You know what, baby, I was a fool to be embarrassed by you. You're fine, and you're one of my best friends. You're also the love of my life, and I love you. I'll be proud to be seen with you." He pulled out the jewelry box from his back pocket, then opened it for her to see. "Amy! Will you marry me?"

She cried heavily while covering her mouth with one hand. "Oh my god, how did you and how could you afford that ring? Yes," she answered. People standing around watching all began clapping as the new husband and wife were holding one another tightly.

The end

CPSIA information can be obtained
at www.ICGtesting.com
Printed in the USA
BVHW071433021222
653300BV00004B/254